"Will Santa skip us this year because he doesn't know we're at a hotel instead of our old, burned-up house?"

Dylan swallowed, his heart aching for the child's worries. The boys wouldn't fully understand how much they'd lost in the fire for a while—the memories and surety that they would always be safe.

"We'll leave a note at our old house with a cookie and some milk," the boy's twin brother said, and a smile replaced his worried look.

The children's parents turned to Dylan and Jenna. "Thank you for all you're doing for us. It's so hard…to accept help."

Jenna reached over and squeezed her hand, a warm smile on her face. "When you're back on your feet, you can pay it forward, help someone else who's going through a tough time. That way, the help keeps moving."

Dylan stared at Jenna. Who was this woman and what had she done with the real Jenna Scott?

The waitress took their order, and soon the twins

Books by Dana Corbit

Love Inspired

A Blessed Life
An Honest Life
A New Life
A Family for Christmas
"Child in a Manger"
On the Doorstep
Christmas in the Air
"Season of Hope"
A Hickory Ridge Christmas
Little Miss Matchmaker
Homecoming at Hickory Ridge
*An Unexpected Match
*His Christmas Bride

*Wedding Bell Blessings

DANA CORBIT

Dana Corbit started telling "people stories" at about the same time she started forming words. So it came as no surprise when the Indiana native chose a career in journalism. As an award-winning newspaper reporter and features editor, she had the opportunity to share wonderful true-life stories with her readers. She left the workforce to be a homemaker, but the stories came home with her as she discovered the joy of writing fiction. The winner of the 2007 Holt Medallion competition for novel writing, Dana feels blessed to share the stories of her heart with readers.

Dana lives in southeast Michigan, where she balances the make-believe realm of her characters with her equally exciting real-life world as a wife, carpool coordinator for three athletic daughters and food supplier for two disinterested felines.

His Christmas Bride
Dana Corbit

Steeple
Hill®

Published by Steeple Hill Books™

STEEPLE HILL BOOKS

Steeple
Hill®

Recycling programs
for this product may
not exist in your area.

ISBN-13: 978-0-373-87568-9

HIS CHRISTMAS BRIDE

www.SteepleHill.com

Printed in U.S.A.

And Jesus looked at them and said,
"With men it is impossible, but not with God;
for all things are possible with God."
—*Mark* 10:27

To the Baxter boys—Brock, Dylan and Logan—
who have inspired my fictional stories in more
ways than just by lending me your names. You are
all amazing young men, who I'm sure will be
real-life heroes in the future. Also, to Melissa,
my own Amy Warren. And, as always, to the
POTLs, the six amazing women who inspire and
push me to tell stories from my heart.

Chapter One

The house looked like a fire-department statistic just waiting to happen. Either that or the trigger for a power outage the likes of which southern Indiana had never known. Jenna Scott couldn't decide which as she tromped up the walk toward the redbrick colonial, passing a riot of Christmas lights and a holiday amusement park along the way.

On one side of the walk, a half-scale crèche rested serenely on the lawn with animals, shepherds and wise men focused on the Christ child. On the other side, a trio of plastic carolers sang a scratchy version of "O Little Town of Bethlehem," and a herd of mechanical reindeer bent to munch on artificial snow.

Could someone say "over the top"?

Her mother hadn't been exaggerating when she'd mentioned that the Warrens' Christmas display was "a sight to behold." The celebration was also another excuse for best friends and matchmakers Trina Scott and Amy Warren to force their adult children together.

They'd been campaigning for an event like this ever since the Scott-Warren matrimonial merger six months before. Jenna figured that whatever the evening held in store for her personally, it promised to be entertaining.

As she stepped to the door, decorated in green-foil gift wrap, a hum of voices spilled from inside, competing with Elvis bellowing "Blue Christmas."

"So much for a quiet Christmas at home," she told the life-size Santa doll that smiled at her from a wicker chair on the porch.

Suddenly that bah-humbug spirit filled her again, making the winter wonderland feel claustrophobic. It was only the second Christmas since her father died, and she doubted it would be any easier than last year. Visiting Markston wasn't like coming home for the holidays, anyway. Markston wasn't her home. Nowhere was, really.

Someone yanked open the door before she had the chance to knock, and Jenna found herself wrapped in a hug warm enough to cut through the December freeze.

"Jenna, dear, you finally made it," Mrs. Warren said.

She stepped out of the woman's embrace, glancing back at the outdoor decorations. "Wow. This is great."

"I'm glad you like it. Now come in out of the cold before you catch your death." Already Amy Warren was pulling Jenna into the entry where the rest of the Scotts and Warrens were gathered. Just being in the house again made butterflies flutter in her stomach.

Her mother gripped her in a tight hug. "We thought you'd never get here."

"I told you my flight would get in after dinner, and I came straight from the airport." Jenna gestured toward the deep-blue airline-attendant uniform she'd been wearing since she'd left her apartment that morning in Romulus, Michigan, and headed to Detroit Metro.

"It doesn't matter now because we're all here together again," Trina told her.

"All here?" Jenna asked.

She scanned the faces of the other guests waiting to greet her. Newlyweds Matthew Warren and her younger sister, Haley, smiled over at her, Matthew's four-year-old daughter, Lizzie, resting on his hip. Jenna's other sister, Caroline, stood next to them, and the youngest Warren brother, Logan, was there, as well, but appeared to be inching toward the door.

They were not *all* there—the one member of the Warren family she'd hoped most to see was missing: Dylan. He was the whole reason she'd agreed to participate in this joint holiday celebration in the first place. The whole reason she hadn't canceled the trip and stayed in Michigan.

"Am I missing something?"

Jenna startled at the sound coming from behind her, butterflies continuing their mad dance inside her belly. Taking a deep breath, she turned toward the gruff voice she would have recognized anywhere. Leaning over the staircase railing with his wavy brown hair falling forward on his forehead was the best friend she'd ever had. The one who'd left a hole in her life when he'd removed himself from it.

For the space of a few breaths, she could only look up at him, following the lines of his face and settling on his warm chocolate eyes. Those eyes were amazing. If he were anyone else besides Dylan Warren...Jenna blinked, surprised by the strange path her thoughts had taken. But this was Dylan, even if the passing years had put more granite in the chiseled cheekbones, which had always contradicted his teddy-bear personality. His smile probably would look as friendly and unassuming as it always had…if he was smiling. He wasn't.

"Hey, Dylan," she choked out over the knot that had formed in her throat. "Oh, I mean, Dr. Dylan." Now that he'd finished his doctor of optometry degree at Indiana University and had joined a local optometry practice, he'd earned that title, even if he didn't look much like a medical professional now in a tan flannel shirt and jeans.

"Hi." He cleared his throat. "Dylan's fine."

Only Dylan didn't appear to be fine. He didn't even make eye contact with her as he shuffled down the stairs and joined the others in living room. Her heart sank.

Jenna didn't know what she'd expected. That when he saw her, the four years of distance and the misunderstanding that caused them would fall away so they could resume their friendship as if it had only been a pause in their conversation? Hadn't the awkwardness between them last summer at Matthew and Haley's wedding clued her in that it wouldn't be so easy? But she'd wished, anyway.

She couldn't allow herself to be discouraged, though, not when she'd prayed for a chance to try to make it up to Dylan for the day she'd treated his feelings so cavalierly. This visit might be the chance she'd hoped for.

Four years ago, she'd excused her actions by telling

herself she hadn't realized that their plans had been firm, let alone that he'd thought it was a real date, instead of just hanging out. Now she saw that situation—saw a lot of things—through new eyes.

Before she could say anything, Jenna was swallowed in one of those Warren-Scott hug fests where she couldn't distinguish one form from the next in the crush. She couldn't be sure, but she didn't believe Dylan was among those who hugged her.

"Now that we're all here," Amy Warren began after all the greetings ended, "we need to get started on the Christmas festivities."

"Yeah, we'd better hurry up and get started before Easter comes and we've missed it," Logan piped up, earning a frown from his mother and a few chuckles from the others.

Jenna realized she was looking again at Dylan and quickly began to scan the indoor holiday decorations. Too much of a good thing was the only way she could describe the pine garland that was draped over every stair railing, curtain rod and windowsill.

The coffee table had been transformed into a miniature Christmas village. Several manger scenes and a Madonna figurine covered other tables and shelves. The individual pieces were lovely, but when compiled this way, they created a frenzied feeling in the room, which did nothing to help Jenna calm her nerves.

"The only thing missing is a tree," Jenna breathed.

Logan tapped his head as if she'd just given him a great idea. "Good thing we're going to the Christmas-tree farm to cut one down."

Jenna turned to her mother and raised an eyebrow.

Now the way Dylan and the others were dressed and the line of hiking boots by the door made sense.

"Didn't I mention we'd be tree hunting tonight?" Her mother wore a sheepish grin.

"No, you didn't. Anyway, didn't you look at the weather forecast?"

"The rain isn't expected until after midnight."

Caroline stepped closer to Jenna. "Mom didn't warn me, either. She only said we would be participating in the Warren family's Christmas traditions this year to celebrate the new connection between our families."

Jenna nodded, having heard the same story. She hadn't been thrilled with the idea of sharing in another family's holiday traditions. Her own family's celebrations had been portable at best because of her father's frequent corporate relocations. She'd needed no reminder of how their wreaths and ornaments had hung in different family rooms every year or so.

Jenna glanced over to where the middle Warren brother stood. Dylan would understand those bittersweet memories. He'd been her only constant after each of her family's moves—only a phone call or a text message away. But as she watched him now, his attention was focused on something in the family room, as if he hadn't heard the conversation. Or didn't care.

"Come in here," Amy Warren said as she ushered them into the room where Dylan had been looking. "Then I'll give you our agenda."

Jenna followed gamely as Amy led them toward the huge sectional sofa. She took her place on one end, noting that Dylan sat at the opposite end.

Amy stood in the center of the L-shaped couch as

if leading a class. "Okay, we'll begin with tonight's tree cutting. Reverend Boggs and his wife, Lila, were supposed to join us, but he called to say something came up at church."

"Did he say if everything was okay?" Matthew asked. As an attorney who also worked as the weekend music minister at Community Church of Markston, he was usually in the loop regarding most church matters.

"He only said they would catch up with us here later." Mrs. Warren sent a glance Jenna's way, noting her outfit. "We have clothes for you upstairs."

"See how well they outfitted me?" Caroline modeled a red flannel shirt with sleeves that hung off her hands.

"Is that how Dylan's shirt fits you?" Trina asked her daughter, a secretive smile playing on her lips.

"Quit it, Mom," Caroline warned in a low voice.

"I'm not doing anything."

"Keep it that way."

No one could blame Caroline for being cautious after their mothers tried to arrange a match between Caroline and Matthew Warren last spring, only to have Matthew and Haley fall in love, instead. Caroline wouldn't appreciate any more shenanigans from their two moms with their ridiculous plan to arrange marriages among their children.

Their matchmaking attempt this time was particularly funny. Jenna's type-A, corporate-ladder-climbing-retail-executive sister matched with quirky, laid-back Dylan Warren? That was enough to pull the smirk right off her face: she didn't like the idea of Dylan being set up with Caroline.

It was a fleeting, silly thought, but as Jenna tucked

it away, a more powerful musing settled into its place. Their meddling mothers had already enjoyed one success in their matchmaking scheme, which they'd always jokingly referred to as The Plan. Did their achievement mean they would up their games now? Would they be able to convince Dylan and Caroline that their mothers knew best, no matter what their initial objections? She tried to picture herself at Dylan and Caroline's wedding and almost had to leave the room. She didn't like this. She didn't like it one bit.

Tonight was even tougher than Dylan had expected it would be. The prospect of having Jenna Scott in town for an interminable two weeks had already scored high on his dread scale, but the combination of sitting in the same room as Jenna *and* listening to his mother tell them her plans for another dysfunctional Warren family Christmas had topped even that.

Both reminded him of things he could never have. Both evoked humiliating memories best left in the past.

"Remember, tree trimming is only the beginning," Amy told her captive audience, rubbing her hands together like a child waiting to open her Christmas presents. "Tomorrow we'll start the cooking and baking. First the treats and then the pierogi and cabbage rolls."

Dylan felt tired, and they weren't even elbow-deep in cookie dough yet. Christmas always had been a trying experience for Dylan and his brothers. Their mother had made each celebration bigger, better and brighter than the last as she tried to make up for her husband's absence in the boys' lives. Dylan knew from experience that nothing could make up for that.

Now his mother wanted to share the humiliating, sideshow event with the new in-laws. She acted as if the two families had been joined in marriage, instead of just his older brother and Jenna's baby sister. If only he could have found another optometry conference to attend, he could have avoided this year's festivities and the holiday guests with a legitimate-sounding excuse.

When his mother started describing the thirty or so goodie platters they would make for church friends and neighbors, Dylan cleared his throat.

"You know, Mom, maybe we should consider cutting back on the baking this year. Maybe make fewer platters. Or just give gifts from your bakery."

"Give gifts from the shop?"

From her incredulous tone, he would have thought he'd just suggested giving day-old bread from the supermarket as gifts rather than the scrumptious, designer cakes his mother created at her bakery, Amy's Elite Treats.

"And why would we cut back, anyway?" She waved away his suggestion with a brush of her fingers through the air. "We have more hands in the kitchen this year."

That's the point, he wanted to say. Fewer recipients would mean less baking and less time spent with all those extra hands. "Just a thought."

His mother rolled her eyes, turning back to the group. "Then Monday night we have tickets to the see *The Nutcracker*. Third row." She shot her arm into the air as if she'd just won a medal. "And then we'll take a car tour to see the Festival of Lights."

Dylan's frustration built with each event his mother listed. Why couldn't she see that all this busyness had nothing to do with the true meaning of Christmas? And of all the women in this world, why had Matthew chosen to marry a Scott sister? Okay, he would concede that point. Haley and Matthew were too perfect together for God not to have planned that one.

But if Matthew had married someone else, they could have been enduring these excessive Christmas festivities with another family. Instead of this one. Now he would have to spend a miserable holiday trying to avoid the one person who'd always been able to send his stable life crumbling into invisible fault line: Jenna. Always Jenna.

She represented his life's biggest disappointment—the person he'd always loved who'd always been out of reach. She'd made him question everything he knew to be true: his values and even his faith. How could he not when he'd always been so certain that God intended them to be together? Even now, after working as hard to forget her as he had to finish his degree, he could no more prevent his gaze from shifting her way than he could have given time a lunch break.

At twenty-six, she looked impossibly young with all that caramel-colored hair wrangled into a long ponytail. The only difference between the way she'd worn it in junior high and the style now was the longer bangs off to one side. Her face was thinner now, too, but that only magnified the impact of the high cheekbones and generous lips that were Scott family traits. She was painfully, perfectly beautiful.

Stop. He looked from side to side to be certain he hadn't said that aloud. After four years he should have been unaffected by those eyes, the color of iced tea, and that skin, like a porcelain doll.

He hated that she still had such an effect on him. Why, around her, had he always been like a kid with a milk allergy who couldn't resist a scoop of ice cream? Would he ever be able to look at her and feel innocuous familiarity and nothing more? Because the answer to that question could incriminate him, Dylan was grateful to Jenna for the night she'd pressed his hand regarding their friendship.

It wasn't the first time Jenna had behaved selfishly—far from it—but it was different from the rest. After he'd spent months scraping up the courage to ask her on a date, he'd finally asked and she'd accepted. Then, as he was leaving for his five-hour trip to the Michigan State campus to meet her, she'd called to reschedule their "buddies' weekend" because some rugby player had asked her to a movie.

In that moment, when the proverbial straw broke the camel's back, he'd told her he was finished with her. He wouldn't be her friend anymore. If not for that night, he might still be there, serving as her long-suffering best friend and always wishing for more.

"Dylan, are you listening?"

He shifted, glancing up to see his mother watching him, her arms crossed over her chest. "Sure, Mom." At least he was now.

"After church Sunday, we can get started on the Christmas-ornament project." Amy turned to explain to the Scotts. "We do one every year. We need to find a new service project, too."

She paused finally, tapping her head with her index finger as though wondering if she'd forgotten anything. "Oh. Right. Rehearsal for Christmas Eve services. It's our tradition to sing together in the choir, and I'm sure Matthew could use the extra voices."

Matthew appeared apologetic as he turned to his wife's sisters. "I can always use every available voice." He took his new bride's hand. "I've already recruited one Scott sister for the choir."

"As if I had a choice," Haley offered with a wink.

"Now for the events on Christmas Day," his mother began again.

Amy Warren must not have heard Logan's sigh because she prattled on, describing the elaborate Christmas dinner they would share. Dylan tuned out again, his attention pulled by something as strong as gravity toward the face he had no business looking at, the person who was toxic to his best interests.

Jenna caught his gaze this time, pink lips lifting in a tentative grin. Ignoring the jolt he would probably always feel when she smiled at him, he turned away from her and focused on his mother again. Jenna wanted things between them to be the same as they'd always been. She'd made that clear enough in a few letters and during a stilted conversation at the wedding. But their relationship could never be the same.

They were different people. At least he was. He was an adult now, a respected member of the Markston community, not the everyman she'd found so easy to overlook. And this new Dylan Warren refused to allow Jenna Scott to get under his skin again.

Dylan planned to keep his distance from her during this visit just as he had for the past four years, just as he had at the wedding. Although he still felt guilty for using his graduate studies as an excuse to avoid going to Michigan for her father's funeral nearly two years before, he couldn't think about that now, not when he needed to focus on giving her a wide berth during her visit. If he could avoid caving in to her attempts to get close to him for the next two weeks, maybe he could finally exorcise her from his heart for good and get on with his life.

His plan in place, Dylan sneaked another look at Jenna to test his resolve. Immediately he realized his mistake. As she listened to his mother's speech, Jenna had tilted her head to the side, revealing a long expanse of her elegant neck above the collar of her uniform. The impulse to brush her skin there was so strong that Dylan had to fist his hands and turn away to shake it. He was in trouble, and he knew it. If he wanted to have any hope of maintaining his distance from Jenna Warren this Christmas season, he needed to start praying for strength right now and keep right on doing it through the New Year.

Chapter Two

Dylan slipped out of his muddy hiking boots and gave his head a hard shake, sending droplets of water from his hair flying every which way. Dripping less than he had before, he stepped through his mother's front door.

"I'd like to see a Currier & Ives painting of that precious holiday scene," he groused.

"I heard that, Dylan Thomas." His mother came down the hallway and handed him a towel.

"Sorry, Mom." He toweled off his hair.

He didn't know how his mother could still call her twenty-six-year-old son by both his names when he annoyed her, any more than he could understand how she was still in a festive mood after such a disastrous tree-cutting outing. It had begun to sprinkle the moment they'd pulled up at the tree farm, and by the time they'd left with that gigantic, soggy Scotch pine, Dylan had been looking around for animals lined up two by two.

Matthew opened the storm door and stuck his head inside, raindrops running down the lenses of his glasses. "Hey, little brother, we could use a hand out here. We're setting up the tree in the garage so it can dry out."

Dropping the towel on the tile, Dylan retrieved his boots and followed his brother. So much for his much-needed break from being around Jenna.

"Any chance Mom's decided to cut festivities short tonight?" Matthew asked over his shoulder.

"Are you kidding? She and your mother-in-law already have the hot chocolate simmering on the stove, and I could hear their bad duet of 'We Wish You a Merry Christmas' as soon as I walked in the house."

"I figured we wouldn't get out of it," Matthew said. "Never let it be said that a little rain could keep our mom from her holiday celebration."

"At least you aren't the newest matchmaking target."

Matthew laughed the laugh of someone who'd been there. "Stay strong, brother."

As they stepped into the garage, Caroline and Jenna were holding the tree upright while Logan crouched below, twisting the braces of the tree stand into its trunk.

"Could you two hold that thing straight?" Logan called up from the bottom.

"Come on, Nature Boy, don't you know how to deal with trees once they're cut down?" Caroline chided.

"I can with some proper help. Who cut this trunk, anyway? It's crooked."

Jenna caught Dylan's eye and laughed, and even he couldn't resist smiling at that. Logan, the resident park ranger among them, had cut the tree himself. They rested it on its side so Logan could even up the trunk and remove the lowest branches. Then, with several hands and a lot of grumbling, they finally secured the tree in its stand with only a slight lean.

Their work finished, they filed into the house, leaving their boots and soaked coats near the door.

"Everyone in here," Trina told them, ushering them into the family room, where Amy sat on the edge of the brick hearth.

Although they'd had only minutes to put the party together, the mothers had risen to the occasion. Now orange and yellow flames danced in the gas fireplace, strains of recorded Christmas carols filtered from the stereo speakers, and a spread of finger sandwiches and snacks rested on the side table. And because no Warren-Scott gathering would be complete without them, two of his mother's famous cakes were arranged on cake stands.

They were preparing to say grace when the doorbell rang, and Matthew hurried to let Reverend Leyton Boggs and his wife inside. They conferred in hushed voices as they hung up their coats and then made their way into the family room, their faces stoic.

"Is everything all right, Reverend?" Amy Warren asked.

The minister smiled in that comforting way he'd used in every memorial service Dylan had ever attended. Something was wrong.

"Late this afternoon, there was a fire downtown that destroyed a young family's home," Reverend Boggs began. "Brad and Kelly Denton were already struggling since Brad was laid off from his job, and their car wasn't running, so this fire came at a particularly tough time. The home was rented, and they had no insurance."

"How awful for them," Jenna said. "Do they have children?"

Lila Boggs nodded. "Two boys. Seven-year-old twins named Connor and Ryan. But praise God, they all got out safely."

"Yes, praise Him for that." The minister told how the Dentons had been trying to provide at least a simple Christmas for their sons, only to have their few gifts go up in flames along with the rest of their possessions.

Empathetic murmurs filled the room as the minister told more of the specifics. But Dylan barely heard the details. The story made him so uncomfortable that he found it hard to sit still. A family already limping along through life now had the burden and indignity of being homeless at Christmas. He'd heard dozens of those tragic holiday stories before, but this one touched him in a special way.

It had to be the mention of those two little boys that spoke to him. His heart ached as he imagined the confusion they had to feel after today's events, after the security blankets of home and safety had been ripped from them. He'd known a day like that once himself: the day his father left. At twelve years old, he'd been older than these boys, but he remembered how powerless and small he'd felt. How frightened he'd been that his world would never the right again. Now he grieved for these children, who'd lost their childhood just as he had.

"I spoke with the Dentons by phone, and then Lila and I drove them to the Markston Inn for the night. I paid for their night's stay with church emergency-relief funds," Reverend Boggs was saying when Dylan tuned back in to the conversation.

"But they're going to need more than temporary help. We've offered on behalf of the church to adopt this family through the holidays, so I'll be seeking support from church members like yourselves…" He let his words trail away as he waited for someone to step up to the challenge.

"Of course, we'll help," Dylan's mother answered. "We've been looking for a Christian service project, so we'll make a donation."

"That's a great idea," Logan said, and the others chimed in their agreement.

"I knew I could count on the Warrens and, of course, the Scotts." The minister smiled. "I'm sure this young family will appreciate whatever you can give."

Neither the accolades nor his mom's best chocolate walnut torte sat well with Dylan tonight. He felt as if they were all taking the easy way out—himself included. What they were willing to offer just didn't feel like enough.

Reverend Boggs glanced at the wall clock. "Some Indianapolis news vans were at the scene of the fire, so the story should make the ten-o'clock news."

"Hey, somebody turn it on," Logan called out.

Dylan stretched toward the sofa table and retrieved the remote, flicking on the flat-screen television in the corner.

"The holidays will be a little less bright for a young Markston family who narrowly escaped tragedy today when a blaze broke out in their northside rental home," said a reporter whose bright red coat appeared too festive for the somber news.

As the reporter continued her story, the camera panned first to the smoldering structure and then to the couple and their sons, huddled together in the chilly rain with blankets draped over their shoulders.

No longer hungry, Dylan set his plate aside. The story had been stirring enough, but to put faces to the tragedy brought the sad situation right into the family room. He'd pictured those children in his mind, but on the screen they appeared smaller than he'd imagined. Defenseless. Their bright eyes peeked out from beneath their parents' arms as they watched the firefighters wage a losing battle with the blaze.

Stark reality was clear on Brad and Kelly Denton's faces. Dylan remembered that his mother wore an expression like that during the early days after his father left. Matthew had looked that same way after his first wife had deserted him and Lizzie. The Dentons might have escaped with their lives, but the young couple, like his mother and his brother, had been unable to protect their children from life's unfortunate truths.

In the next shot the reporter was standing with the family, all of them under the shelter of two large umbrellas. Brad Denton squeezed the boy next to him and said, "We feel blessed that we all got out safely. As long as we're together, we'll figure out the rest."

Dylan could only stare at the screen. He'd been feeling sorry for himself all night when people like the Dentons, who had real problems and every right to their own pity party, were counting their blessings. He'd forgotten to count his.

Around him the room had fallen silent as the news broadcast moved to commercial break.

"It's a sad story," Reverend Boggs began again as Dylan shut off the television. "Still, I feel God has a blessing planned here. I'm sorry to run, but I need to call some of the other church members."

"It won't be necessary to make any more calls, Reverend." Dylan waited as the others turned their surprised expressions his way. He couldn't blame them—he wasn't usually the idea man in this crowd, but he had to be this time. No one else was stepping forward, and he couldn't turn his back on those little boys.

"Look at all of us." He held his hands wide to indicate the size of the group. "Sure, we can write a check, but I think we can do a lot more." Out of the corner of his eye, Dylan could see Jenna watching him, a strange expression on her face. He pressed on. "Between our two families, we should volunteer to adopt the Dentons ourselves."

Everyone spoke up at once—that is, everyone except Jenna. She was too busy staring at Dylan, who didn't sound at all like the Dylan she'd once called her best friend. Who was this take-charge guy? *Her* Dylan would have been more than happy to let other people make plans and then join in for the ride.

That he'd spoken aloud the exact idea she'd been bouncing around in her head surprised her even more. How could they not do more for that poor family? Her worries about reconnecting with Dylan seemed small when compared to those of these young parents who had no place to live and no way to feed and clothe their children. It wasn't right for her to warm herself by the fire while this family had been huddled under blankets, trying to shield their children from the cold.

"He's right," Matthew said, his voice rising above

the rest. "We have so much. We don't need anything for Christmas. The Dentons will need everything."

"That's a great idea," Haley chimed in.

"We have to help them," Jenna told them. Her throat clogged with emotion as she tried to put herself in the shoes of those young parents. She could only imagine the hopelessness they felt.

Mrs. Warren stood up, shaking her head. "I don't know. That's a big project you're taking on, Dylan. We can help, but it might be better if we spread the load among various church members." She frowned as if realizing more pitfalls. "And we would have to cancel some of our holiday plans—"

"Not cancel, Mom," Dylan said, standing beside her and wrapping his arm around her shoulders. "Just tweak. Remember, you wanted us to spend quality time with the Scotts during the holidays, and what could be better than spending that time helping others?"

"We wanted to share our Christmas traditions, too." Mrs. Warren's face fell in disappointment.

"And we will," Dylan assured her. "Some of them."

"We already have," Logan said. "We found the tree."

Mrs. Warren shrugged as she sat on the hearth. "If you're sure we can handle that much work…"

"Of course we can." Dylan nodded as if to emphasize his words. His mother's reticence appeared to surprise him. Jenna, too, found the woman's reaction strange. Mrs. Warren was one of the most kind-hearted people she knew, so Jenna assumed something else was bothering her.

"What did you have in mind?" Matthew asked after a long pause.

"We could put some of the money and effort we would have used for Mom's great list of activities toward making Christmas bright for someone else."

Although Dylan glanced his mother's way, the first response came from someone smaller.

"Do we have to give away our Christmas tree?" Lizzie asked, her eyes sad.

"Of course not, silly." Dylan crossed the room and scooped up his niece. "But don't you think that other family should have a nice Christmas, too?"

When she nodded, he tugged on one of her braids and lowered her to the floor. Jenna couldn't help smiling at the sweet gesture. Dylan really seemed to adore Lizzie. The two of them had been so inseparable at the wedding that Jenna had been ashamed to be jealous of a child.

He turned to the minister. "Now, Reverend, you and Mrs. Boggs have met the Dentons. Can you give us an idea of what their needs are?"

"You'll need to start with the basics. Food, clothing and shelter. Lila and I are planning to meet with the family for breakfast tomorrow morning to find out the specifics. We wanted them to rest tonight."

Dylan nodded. "Would you mind if a few of us joined you so you could introduce us?"

"That might be best," Lila answered for her husband.

"You should go, Dylan." Matthew gestured toward him from the sofa. "This was your idea."

Dylan appeared surprised by his older brother's suggestion, but he nodded. He was probably as used to Matthew assuming plans in his family as Jenna was with Caroline taking over organizational duties in theirs.

"I would like to go."

He smiled that boyish Dylan smile that Jenna had missed while he'd been dodging her efforts to talk to him all evening. He hadn't been mean exactly, unless treating her as if she was invisible counted as mean. She marveled at his compassion for the Dentons. She could only hope that one day he would send some of that kindness her way and finally forgive her.

Jenna realized that she'd never thought to appreciate Dylan for the gift he was. She wished he would give her the chance to tell him how sorry she was for that and to show him she wasn't the same selfish person he used to know. God had made sure of that change.

"Who else would like to join us for breakfast?" Reverend Boggs asked as he took a seat next to his wife.

Jenna's mother spoke up. "Caroline should go."

Caroline was already shaking her head when Matthew offered a suggestion.

"Jenna should go. She and Dylan are buddies, and they haven't seen each other in a while."

Matthew probably thought he was helping his brother out by offering him an escape from their mothers' matchmaking efforts, but Dylan looked like a man stuck between two unacceptable choices and hoping for a third.

Jenna jumped in before he found one. "That sounds great. I'd love to have the chance to meet the Dentons."

She knew better than to look at Dylan because his gaze wouldn't be tossing daisies at her. Dylan probably thought she'd only accepted Matthew's suggestion to get the chance to spend time with him, but it was more than that. The Denton family's story had touched her, too, and she wanted to reach out to them.

"That's fine," Dylan said finally, but he didn't look at her. Instead, he grabbed a legal pad out of the drawer in his mother's roll-top desk.

"We'll know more tomorrow, but we can divide up the general areas now. Housing, furniture, clothing and food." He wrote as he spoke. "If we split into teams, we'll be able to accomplish more."

"They should be teams of two, one from each family," Jenna said the moment the idea popped into her head. "I'll work with Dylan."

"Wait." Amy exchanged a glance with Trina before she turned back to Dylan. "I thought it might be nice if you worked with—"

Caroline stood to interrupt. "I'd like to get the chance to spend time with my new brother-in-law." She turned to Matthew. "Okay with you?"

"Fine with me."

"I'll work with Jenna, then."

Although Dylan's tone might have been more enthusiastic if he'd just volunteered to clean Porta-Johns, Jenna was pleased to have won the point. He would probably raise eyebrows if he refused to work with her.

Dylan teamed up the remaining family members, pairing his mother with Jenna's mother, and Logan with Haley. Because the youngest Warren brother and the youngest Scott sister had been like oil and water together ever since they were in diapers, he assigned Lizzie to work with them to keep the peace. That complete, he started dividing the work.

"I had planned to deal with food, but since I'm

working with the premier shopper—" Dylan paused, glancing Jenna's way "—we'll take clothing, toiletries and Christmas gifts."

The minister stood and crossed the room to collect his coat. "Well, Dylan, it looks as if you have this under control. I'll have to remember your organizational skills the next time we need a new committee leader at church."

Jenna agreed with the minister's praise and would have said so, but the look Dylan sent her way made her keep her opinion to herself. Her plan of working on a team with him didn't seem like such a great idea, after all. Did she really think forcing him to be with her would help her to restore their friendship?

No, she'd gone about this the wrong way. Instead of approaching him slowly and letting him remember why they once were close, she'd forced her way into his space, reminding him of how selfish she'd always been. She'd wanted to prove to him she was different, and all she'd done was show him more of the same.

What was she supposed to do now? Once again, she'd messed things up with Dylan, but she would just have to work within the uncomfortable situation she'd created. She'd committed to helping the Dentons, and she intended to follow through with her commitment. Maybe if Dylan saw that, he would eventually be able to forgive her, after all.

Chapter Three

Brad Denton looked as uncomfortable as a cowboy in a tuxedo as he took a seat next to his wife at Home Cooking Café the next morning. Well, Dylan could relate to his discomfort. As if it wasn't awkward enough meeting the Dentons for the first time, Jenna was sitting next to him. He wished he could ignore her, but the coconut scent of her shampoo invaded his senses every time she turned her head, and the chime of her laughter filtered into his ears. If only his senses hadn't picked today to become sharp enough to detect a noise in the next room or hear a butterfly fluttering its wings.

He'd counted on her being a no-show this morning—like all the other times—but that hadn't worked out for him, either. Why she'd picked this morning to come through on one of her commitments, he wasn't sure. She wasn't doing anything halfway, either. They'd barely made it to their seats, and she was already playing hostess, chatting with Lila Boggs and Kelly Denton.

"Do you think we should send out a search party for the boys?" Reverend Boggs asked as he opened his menu.

Brad glanced over his shoulder toward the restroom where Connor and Ryan had hurried before the hostess could seat them. He spoke conspiratorially to Dylan. "Two more minutes and we're going in."

The men's room door opened then, and the boys rushed out, saving the adults from that covert mission. The boys hurried across the room, looking like matching wind-up toys, not technically running—their mother had warned them not to—but close to it.

As the twins scrambled into the two remaining seats at the long table, mischievous grins on their faces, Dylan's thoughts cleared. He remembered why they were all working together in the first place: for the sake of these little boys. He'd only just met them, and already they inspired a fierce protectiveness in him.

Dylan couldn't get over the fact that Connor and Ryan were laughing and playing as if they'd already forgotten about yesterday's fire and were ready for their next adventure. Children were definitely resilient. He knew from experience. But he also knew that they scarred just as deeply as anyone else did.

Those boys and their parents deserved the best his family and the Scotts could offer, and nothing—not even Jenna—should distract him from giving it.

"I sure hope after all that time in there that you two washed your hands," Kelly said to her sons.

"We did, Mommy." Only one of them answered, but they both held up their hands.

The waitress took their order, and soon the twins

were wolfing down their waffles as if they hadn't eaten in months. Not true, of course, since their parents had already mentioned the pizza they'd eaten in their hotel room late last night.

"Boys, you need to slow down. This isn't a race," Kelly admonished them as she set her fork aside.

Dylan shook his head. "Obviously you weren't a boy who grew up with brothers. In my house, everything was a race or a contest."

"I can vouch for that," Jenna told them. "The Warren brothers competed over who could spit the farthest or cross his eyes the longest, even who had the most ear wax."

Because Dylan couldn't help smiling at the shared memory, he was glad she wasn't looking his way. But she would know about those things. She'd been there for many of those contests and other incidents. He remembered clearly just how important it was to him to win when Jenna was around.

"You really do understand our boys, then," Brad said.

"It sounds as if you've known each other a long time." Kelly looked back and forth between them, searching for a connection.

"Since birth...or a little before," Jenna said, smiling.

"Our mothers are best friends, so they stuck us kids together a lot."

He hadn't intended the comment to sound so harsh, but he failed, and an awkward silence settled over the table. He suddenly felt bad—he didn't want to hurt Jenna. He just didn't want to get pulled back into a friendship that had caused him so much pain. But being around her brought back so many memories, most filled with laughter rather than sadness. It confused and frustrated him that though he knew he should steer clear of her for his own good, part of him was willing to be drawn in again. It didn't do any good for him to wish he could have found an excuse not to work on a team with Jenna. He simply had to work with the situation as it was.

"Anyway...I think we've addressed all the details." Dylan glanced down at the list of tasks in front of him and then to the list of clothing and shoe sizes next to Jenna's coffee cup. "Can any of you think of anything we haven't covered?"

"Will Santa miss us this year because he doesn't know we're at a hotel, instead of our old, burned-up house?" Ryan asked, suddenly serious.

Dylan swallowed, his heart aching for the child's distress. The twins' concerns might not have been as obvious as those of their parents, but they were there.

The adults glanced at one another across the table. The boys wouldn't fully understand how much they'd lost in the fire for a while—the memories and surety that they would always be safe. The grown-ups already knew.

Connor tilted his head to the side. "Do you think Santa will get it if we leave a note for him at our old house to tell him where we are now?"

"As long as we put a cookie and some milk with it." Excitement replaced the worried look on Ryan's face.

"Hey, those are clever ideas, boys." Kelly managed a reassuring smile for her sons.

The waitress stopped by the table to leave the check, and Dylan nabbed it before anyone could look at it. He pulled his wallet from his back pocket and set his credit card with the bill.

Brad glanced at the credit card that represented a free breakfast, and he gripped his hands together. "I don't know if all this is the best idea. Your church has already done so much with the hotel room and all."

Kelly leaned her cheek against her husband's shoulder. All through breakfast, the two of them had been holding hands. "You'll have to forgive my husband. It's hard for him to accept help. We've always made our own way before, and…" As her voice broke, she glanced away, dabbing her eyes with her napkin.

"Pride. It's a tough thing." Brad tried to laugh, but his voice was thick with emotion. "With me out of work and now…this, we're not in a position to be able to turn down help, for the boys at least. So thank you for everything."

"Okay, then," Dylan said. "First we'll—"

Brad rushed on as if Dylan hadn't spoken. "But as soon as we're able, we'll repay every cent."

Reverend Boggs held his hands wide. "Now, Brad, there's no need to worry about that right now. These two families are just trying to do as our Lord directed to feed and clothe those who need it. You would do the same if the situation were reversed. Remember in Matthew 25:40, Jesus said, 'Truly, I say to you, as you did it to one of the least of these my brethren, you did it to me.'"

"It's just hard." Brad shrugged, not quite on board.

In a surprising move, Jenna reached over and squeezed Brad's hand. "Think of it as only tempo-rary." Her smile was warm enough to convince even the most determined person to change his mind. "When you're back on your feet, you can help out somebody else who's going through a tough time. That way the help keeps moving."

When Jenna released his hand, Brad sat straighter in his seat. "Okay. We'll do that."

It was all Dylan could do not to stare at her with his mouth gaping open. He'd never seen her like this before, so generous and selfless, so focused on someone else's need. She was…different.

Don't go there. You can't afford to. Not again.

"That's great." Jenna pushed back from the table and stood. "Now why don't you all get back to the hotel? You probably could use a relaxing day after yesterday. We'll take care of some of these details and have you resettled in no time."

Reacting to her cue, Dylan came to his feet. The others around him stood, as well.

"In no time," he repeated, stepping over to shake hands with Brad.

Jenna was less formal, hugging Kelly first and then bending to offer each of the boys a squeeze. They only grimaced a little.

As she moved on to hug Brad and the minister and his wife, Dylan slanted a perplexed look her way.

He couldn't help but think about how she'd tried to make it easier for the Denton family to accept assistance, seeming to care as much about their feelings as their physical needs. The Jenna he remembered wouldn't have thought to reach out to anyone else. She'd always been too preoccupied as the epicenter of her own universe. But was it possible that she *had* changed.

Again, he forced himself not to read too much into her efforts. She was probably just hurrying the process along so they could finish their charity project and get on with their Christmas activities.

Preoccupied, he didn't see it coming, but Kelly caught up with him, wrapping her arms around him in a fierce hug.

"God bless you for your kindness." Kelly squeezed again and then released him. "Let us know what we can do, We're not afraid of work."

"We definitely will…after you relax today."

Dylan had to admit that Jenna's suggestion was a good one. And he preferred not to have the family present for some of the delicate discussions that might have to take place with additional donors.

He stole another glance at Jenna, who was reassuring the boys about Santa, and his breath caught. Today would be tough. He grimaced. If he was having this much trouble ignoring her with a crowd around them, he couldn't imagine how hard it would be when the two of them were alone together. Maybe if they kept busy the whole time, it wouldn't be so bad. Maybe he could even send her off shopping for clothes while he took on another part of the project. Independent subcommittees, so to speak. Yes, staying busy and dividing duties, that would help. No time to look into her beautiful eyes. No time for her to bring up the day that forced him to put her out of his life. No time for him to change his mind.

Jenna didn't have to look Dylan's way to know he was watching her, instead of the Dentons, as they crossed the parking lot to return to their hotel. The way he'd been studying her the past twenty minutes, she wanted to tell him to turn up the microscope's magnification and take a good look.

She hated guessing that shock was the reason for his sudden curiosity. Was he really so surprised that she'd been kind to the Dentons? Someone would have to be missing a heart not to want to reach out to that great couple and those sweet little boys. Did he believe she was that type of person? Sure, she'd been a little narcissistic in the past, but she couldn't have been that bad. At least she hoped not. And even if she had been, she was different now.

He might not realize it, but she wasn't the only one who'd changed, and from what she'd seen so far, some of his changes hadn't been for the better. He might be this new assertive-doctor type, but where were his sweetness and vulnerability? The qualities that made him Dylan? He was barely recognizable under all of that authoritarian veneer.

Frustration welled up inside her. Dylan would never give her a chance to restore their friendship. She didn't know why she'd ever thought he would. Four years had passed. If he'd wanted to reconnect with her, he would have done it by now, and if she'd expected to have the chance to make amends, she should have tried *before* now.

She didn't want to believe it was too late. Hadn't her mother always told her it was never too late to do the right thing? It had to be the right thing for her to at least apologize for hurting him, whether he forgave her or not. And even if he didn't believe she was the kind of person to think of others, she intended to help the Dentons have the merriest Christmas possible. She had too many blessings in her life not to share them with others.

She would work with Dylan, even if he wasn't happy about working with her. She would pray through the process that they would somehow reconnect. He wasn't the same boy she remembered any more than she was the same girl, but Jenna sensed that buried deep inside him—maybe intentionally hidden from her— was the person she'd once been closer to than anyone else. With God's help, she was determined to find him.

"This is one thing you could have done without me."

At this newest round of Dylan's grousing, Jenna looked over her shoulder at him and grinned. "And have you miss all this?"

She gestured toward the rows of sweaters in the discount store's women's department. He was bored, but if she had agreed to his suggestion that they divide the list of stores and meet up at the end of the day, she wouldn't have had the chance to see him all afternoon. So much for not forcing him to work with her. She sighed. This was getting more complicated by the minute.

"Have some mercy, will you?"

Dylan leaned his elbows on the hand grip of the shopping cart and rubbed his eyes, yawning. They'd already found several outfits and coats for Brad and the boys at the charity clothes closets and resale shops she'd marched him through for hours, but they were purchasing a few clothes for Kelly now. Jenna was in her element, and she wanted her purchases to be just right.

"Okay. I'll be finished here in a minute." She made her final selections and dropped them in the cart. "How does someone so impatient survive a job where you stare at people's eyeballs all day?" she teased.

She would have taken the strange sound he made as a laugh if he'd chuckled at any of her other jokes today.

"Believe me, even just asking, 'Better or worse?' and 'Which is clearer, A or B?' is more interesting than shopping for women's clothes."

He did chuckle that time—at least something had brightened his spirits. He checked his watch again.

"You see," he said, "I was right. At least in this one store we could have gotten more done, faster, if we'd separated and met up at the cash register later."

Jenna frowned as she gathered several items in her arms. "We also would have gotten half as many things for twice as much if we'd done that. Haven't you ever heard of comparison shopping? You can't just march up to the undershirt display and pick the brand with the best commercials. You have to look at price. We only have so much money, and we want to get as much as possible."

"But I could have handled toiletries."

"Probably."

"Probably? How do you think I earned my professional degree? Bid on it on an Internet auction site?"

When she whirled to look at him, Dylan had his arms crossed. Even with his chin tilted up that way, he looked...oddly appealing.

"No. Not the Internet. But can you tell me what kind of shampoo wouldn't sting a kid's eyes or would give long hair like Kelly's a nice shine?"

At first he frowned, but finally he raised his hands in defeat. "Fine. You win."

With this part of their shopping complete, Dylan wheeled the cart out of the women's department and hurried with apparent relief toward Health and Beauty. Jenna had to jog to keep up with his longer stride.

"It wasn't that much of a defeat, was it?" she asked when he finally slowed down in the toothpaste aisle. "What would you know about kids' or women's shampoo? Besides, you always hated to shop. You hated malls, too. Your mom used to bring clothes home for you to try on. She had to return the ones that didn't fit."

"Guilty." He picked up the most expensive tube of cinnamon-flavored toothpaste, but when she lifted her brow, he set it back on the shelf and gestured for her to select one. "But in my defense, malls are just consumer prisons where they pipe in music with subliminal shopping messages and where the lights are so bright they convince you that whatever you're trying on looks good on you."

Jenna picked up a tube of toothpaste next to a sale sign and moved on to the toothbrush display. "Next you're going to tell me about conspiracy theories and grassy knolls."

"A little before my time, don't you think?"

He had smiled at her comment. Finally. A success. She thought back to all the times he'd regaled her with stories from documentaries about the assassination of President John F. Kennedy or the sinking of the *Titanic*, realizing now that she'd only half listened. A better friend would have listened more closely as he spoke about his interests. Note to self, she thought.

Jenna selected two adult toothbrushes on a two-for-one deal and picked two junior-size brushes for the boys. "I still don't understand why you assigned us to the clothes committee when you hate clothes shopping."

Dylan pulled one of the toothbrushes from her hand and tapped her on the head with it. "Are you kidding? How could I not pick the shopping committee when I was working with the crowned queen of shopping? That would have been a waste of your talents."

Jenna laughed, and for a second, it seemed like old times between them as he grinned at her. She smiled in return, and they just stood there for a moment until Dylan seemed to catch himself. He quickly turned away.

Jenna grabbed a container of dental floss and crossed it off on the list before moving on to the razors and shaving cream.

"I bow to your expertise here." She waved toward the merchandise. "Just watch your prices."

"At least I'm good for something here." He pulled shaving cream, a reasonably priced razor and a pack of replacement blades off the shelf, even grabbing a set of disposable razors for Kelly.

"Do these meet your specifications?"

With all the items checked off on this first list, they went through the checkout line and headed to the car. If the others had accomplished as much as she and Dylan had, they were well on their way to a successful project.

"Whew," Dylan said as he pulled on his seat belt. "Now that was an ordeal."

Jenna didn't say anything for a moment. He might think it had been challenging shopping with her, but if he thought that tomorrow she would agree to working separately on different portions of the project, then he had another think coming. They were making progress. She could feel it. And she wasn't going to give up.

"You know we're not done, right?" she asked.

Dylan looked at her with what she hoped was mock dread.

"After we meet with the boys tomorrow to help them write their Santa's lists, we're headed to the mall for Christmas shopping. You better rest up if you thought today was tough."

Dylan groaned and leaned his head on the steering wheel. She reached over, laughing, and gave him a quick pat on the shoulder. He didn't even stiffen at her touch.

Yes, they'd definitely made progress.

Chapter Four

Dylan followed the enthusiastic chatter into his mother's formal dining room. Already from the cars parked outside, he had no doubt they were the last to make it back to the house. And if all that laughter was any indication, they'd all had an enjoyable afternoon.

Had he? He wasn't prepared to answer that question.

Stowing their coats in the closet, Dylan led Jenna down the hall to join the others. Last night he'd wished for any excuse to avoid the family reunion, but now he was anxious to join the crowd. He needed a break from spending time alone with Jenna before he said something he'd regret, something that put him right back where he was before he'd cut her out of his life.

All day he'd tried to work with her and keep his distance at the same time, a tough enough challenge without her making it even harder by being sweet and funny. Combine all that with the fact that he hadn't been able to keep his eyes off her, and he had every reason for the exhaustion he felt now. He'd thought he could tuck away his personal battle and handle the work without breaking a sweat, but compartmentalization like that took practice.

"Aunt Jenna and Uncle Dylan are here," Lizzie announced as they stepped into the doorway. "We went shopping today."

"You did? Did you buy lots of food?" Dylan heard the false-sounding enthusiasm in his voice and grimaced. He would have to try harder if he planned to convince everyone that all was well in his corner of Markston.

"Even yucky stuff like peas."

The look of horror on the child's face had the whole table laughing.

"You're just in time," Amy said as she came through the swinging door from the kitchen, carrying two steaming bowls of Dylan's favorite beef stew.

"Here, Jenna, you sit next to Haley." Amy gestured toward a vacant space. "Dylan, you take your usual spot. We were just about to say grace."

Dylan felt a flash of annoyance when he discovered that he'd been seated next to Caroline and not Jenna. He chose not to dwell on that thought. Caroline acknowledged him with barely a nod. He wasn't the only one who'd realized they were matchmaking targets, and she was keeping her head low.

Matthew's enthusiastic prayer of thanksgiving made him curious, so as soon as he released Caroline's hand on one side and Mrs. Scott's on the other, Dylan leaned forward. "So it sounds like we've had some success today. Does anyone have a report?"

"Why don't you two go first?" Haley suggested. "What were the Dentons like?"

Jenna had just started to take a bite, but she lowered her spoon. Her eyes sparkled as she spoke. "They were amazing. And those boys were so cute. I just wanted to hug them to pieces."

Logan didn't miss a beat. "Haven't they had a hard enough week already?"

The sound of Jenna's laughter made Dylan feel warm inside—too warm. If today was any indication, he'd be crazy by the time the holidays were over. "They even volunteered to help with whatever they can, but I don't know what that would be," he said.

"We know exactly how they can help," Caroline declared before suddenly looking Dylan's way. "I mean…if you think it's a good idea."

Dylan couldn't help but grin. Even the Scott family's resident control freak had given him a vote of confidence. "Okay, what's your plan?"

"Matthew convinced one of his friends to allow the Dentons to stay in one of his rental properties rent-free for one year," Caroline announced.

A chorus of cheers erupted around the table, with Logan throwing in a whoop for good measure.

"That's amazing, you guys." Dylan breathed a contented sigh. If all their plans fell together this easily, they would have the Dentons sipping cocoa by their own fireplace by the first of the week.

Matthew lifted his index finger. "There's one caveat. The house is one of Kevin's new purchases. It's going to require work before it's even inhabitable. Kevin's willing to split the cost on the materials, but we'll have to supply all the elbow grease."

Dylan thought for a minute. This project, which

had started as an exercise in hunting and gathering, had just morphed into an undertaking of brawn and sweat. His mother's warning didn't seem so out of place now. "I guess Brad and Kelly will appreciate having the chance to help."

"Many hands make light work." Mrs. Scott used the old adage she and his mother used to pull out when they were sending their six children off for kitchen duty.

His mother leaned forward in her chair. "So it's a good thing we have ten pairs of willing adult hands."

The others chimed in their agreement, but his mother's response had surprised Dylan the most. "You're right, Mom. With this many hands, we can do anything."

He smiled at her, glad to see she was becoming more interested in the charity project. She hadn't been wild about having her Christmas plans ditched, but he knew better than to think it was because she didn't want to help a family in need. It was just hard for her to give up the Christmas traditions that were so important to her.

"What needs to be done to the house?" Dylan braced himself as he waited for the answer. Although he and his brothers had learned how to repair things like leaky faucets and holes in walls, which were the results of an absentee dad and overenthusiastic wrestling respectively, he wasn't qualified to take on advanced plumbing and electrical work.

"Most of it's cosmetic," Caroline explained. "Just a deep cleaning and some fresh paint. The place was in pretty bad shape when Matthew's friend bought it."

Dylan took reports from the other committees and then asked the two mothers to add researching new and used kitchen appliances to their list, since the house would require them.

"I have a few leads for those things," Mrs. Scott said.

"Speaking of leads," Haley began as she hurried to the living room. She returned holding a few pieces of paper. "They gave us these at the food bank. They're long-term aid sources the Dentons might qualify for. But most won't be available until after the holidays."

"Need doesn't take a holiday," Dylan groused.

"I found the same thing when I checked with a few of my legal clients to see if they had leads on jobs for Brad and Kelly," Matthew said. "Basically nothing until after the New Year."

Dylan shook his head. "Who knew it was so tough to get help?"

"Only the people who really need it."

Until Jenna answered his rhetorical question, Dylan hadn't even realized he'd spoken it aloud. He swallowed as he looked across the table at her. The compassion that filled her eyes tugged at his heart with some unnamed emotion. The connection he'd always felt with her was right there again, but it had shifted somehow. This new, kinder Jenna pulled him in a different way, a way that seemed to be even harder to resist.

The room had become quiet except for the carols filtering from the CD player in the other room. To cut the stillness, Dylan turned to Matthew again. "Hey, thanks for looking into job prospects. I'll check with everyone at church tomorrow and then at work on Monday."

"Oh, right. Work. Some of us aren't on Christmas break this week," Logan joked, earning a frown from Haley, who'd been taking some graduate classes.

"So you two, we're all dying to know how your work went today," Dylan said.

"Us?" Haley asked.

"We got along just fine," Logan retorted.

Lizzie climbed up on her knees in her seat. "But, Mommy, you said Uncle Logan was being ridiculous after he picked up so many cans of ravioli. And Uncle Logan said you picked the bad tuna that trapped dolphins."

Haley didn't get the chance to answer before the room filled with laughter, the solemn mood from moments before having disappeared. Dylan took another look at the others seated around his mother's table. He'd shared a lot of history with the Scott family. He'd hiked down mountain trails, bodysurfed in the Atlantic and taken on the challenges of the newest and fastest roller coasters with Jenna, Haley, Caroline and even Mrs. Scott.

He'd let the painful memories of Jenna obscure the happy times he'd spent with her family. But it didn't have to be that way. He was determined to have a great Christmas with these people he'd known all his life, doing some good and even sharing a few of his mother's traditions. If he could keep things in perspective—and keep his heart under control—maybe these holidays wouldn't be so bad, after all.

The tree looked like a little girl playing dress-up with the contents of her grandma's jewelry case. Okay, an especially tall little girl, Dylan decided, one who wore more strands of lights, glass balls and novelty baubles than any child needed. If that wasn't enough, tinsel clung to the branches like some sort of icing explosion. Despite his determination to enjoy tonight's festivities, Dylan winced at the sight.

After cleaning up dinner together, their families had taken on the challenge of decorating the huge Scotch pine in the living room. Now, as Bing Crosby crooned in the background about the white Christmas they seldom experienced this far south in Indiana, the tree's branches drooped with so much finery he was surprised none of them had broken. After he'd spent the morning with a family who'd lost everything, the holiday display felt like a symbol of excess.

"Isn't it beautiful?" Lizzie stared up at the monstrosity with awe on her face.

"It sure is, honey." Amy gave her granddaughter a squeeze.

"It's amazing, that's for sure." Matthew backed down the ladder he'd used to place the angel on top of the tree.

Dylan tilted his head, trying to see the display from a child's perspective. What kid could resist all those pretty ornaments and lights? He hadn't been able to when he was a little boy. Even now he could pick out a few ornaments that he and his brothers had made in Sunday school or bought for their mother by pooling their quarters. Those pieces represented happy memories, even if they were buried beneath tinsel in the chaos of extremes.

"Well, that's done."

His mother's words brought Dylan back to the present. He turned her way as she brushed off her hands.

"Now we can draw names for the gift exchange," Amy added. "I was thinking we could—"

Dylan held up a hand to stop her. "Wait, Mom. I thought we were going to focus on the Dentons' Christmas, instead of ours. You know, sacrifice a little."

"Believe me, we already have." His mother lifted out her chin, looking offended.

"Sorry, Mom. I know how important all this is to you."

"Do you?"

The sharp question and the frown came from his mother's best friend. Usually Dylan appreciated Mrs. Scott's undying support for his mother, but this time he felt his mother needed to get her priorities straight.

Leaning against the fireplace, Mrs. Scott crossed her arms over her chest. "Do you realize she turned in her third-row *Nutcracker* tickets so they could be resold?"

Dylan coughed into his hand. As a matter of fact, he *hadn't* realized.

"She plans to use those proceeds to add to our project fund."

Jenna spoke up before Dylan had the chance to recover. "That was so nice of you, Mrs. Warren. I'm sure the Dentons will appreciate every sacrifice any of us make."

"Sure glad you think so, Jenna," her mother said. "Because Amy and I returned most of the Christmas gifts we bought for you kids. We have some mall vouchers for you and Dylan to spend when you buy holiday gifts for the Dentons."

"That's a great idea." Jenna looked at Dylan. "I bought mine in Detroit, but most of those stores will be in the mall here, too, so I can return mine. What do you think, Dylan?"

She'd surprised him again with her charitable

gesture. As much as he wanted to help the Dentons, he wished she'd stop saying and doing thoughtful things. If she kept at it, he'd have to leave town for Christmas or risk doing something unwise...like kiss her.

"Sounds good," he managed to reply, pulling his gaze away from her.

"Now can we get back to the exchange?" Amy asked. "Just because we've decided to spend the money we would have used for holiday gifts on our project doesn't mean we can't still have an exchange." She paused for effect, excitement dancing in her eyes again. "This year will be different, though. We'll keep our recipients' names secret until Christmas, and all the gifts must be handmade. Doesn't that sound like fun?"

Lizzie squealed with delight, but the rest of them stayed quiet.

Amy frowned at their lack of enthusiasm. "Now what kind of attitude is that? You mean none of you can handle the challenge of making one gift?"

Matthew held his hands wide. "It isn't that, but—"

"Then but nothing," she finished for him. "Anyway, do you want to disappoint a child at Christmas?"

Amy tilted her head to indicate Lizzie, who must have gotten the hint because she pushed out her lip and batted her lashes.

An "all right," three "fines" and two "okays" later, Amy was smiling again. No one even looked for Mrs. Scott's response, since it was a given that she would agree to whatever plan her friend had in mind.

Crossing to the mantel, Amy pulled off a clear vase filled with red and green glass ornaments and poured its contents on the table. Last to fall out were several strips of white paper, which she stuffed back inside.

"Names for a gift exchange, I presume?" Dylan asked.

"I try to plan ahead. Here, everyone draw a piece of paper and, remember, that name is a secret." She turned to her granddaughter. "Except for Lizzie. She and I will read her paper together, and I'll help her make the gift."

Each took a slip of paper from the vase, and then at Amy's cue, they all unfolded the slips at the same time. When he read the name, Dylan swallowed, trying to keep his expression impassive despite his racing heart. Jenna, of course. He should have known he would draw her name. What were the odds? One in eight if he didn't include the chance he could have chosen his own name.

What would he get her—no, *make* for her? He didn't even know her anymore. A few years ago, he knew her details down to her current favorite in her fickle fragrance collection, but now he didn't know what she liked. The idea of handmade gifts made it more difficult somehow. More personal. *Too* personal. He doubted that one of those pot holders he and his brothers used to make on a plastic loom would fit the bill either.

Dylan stuffed the bit of paper in his pocket. What had he done to deserve a week like this? Wasn't it bad enough that he would be spending several more days working closely with the one woman from whom he most needed to keep his distance? The amazing woman who, he was starting to worry, was destined to keep torturing him, in one way or another, for the rest of his life?

Forget about the two front teeth the old songwriter requested for a Christmas gift—all he wanted this Christmas was a break.

Chapter Five

The next morning Jenna settled into the pew between her sisters, peeking over her shoulder every few seconds to see if the two tardy Warren brothers had arrived. She'd tried to save a seat for Dylan, but her mother and Mrs. Warren clearly had other plans, so she gave up and sat where she was told.

This was the first time she'd attended services at the Community Church of Markston since Matthew and Haley's wedding last June, and the sanctuary looked nothing like the elegant, white-roses scene she remembered. Two huge Christmas trees flanked the choir loft, dozens of poinsettias were gathered on the steps to the podium and greenery and bows were draped along the walls above the stained-glass windows.

Excitement was in the air, anticipation that seemed to be about more than just the retail frenzy that used to be so important to her. All around her, everything appeared to be prepared and waiting for the arrival of the Christ child.

As the organ prelude continued to play and stragglers hurried to their pews, Jenna glanced to the back of the sanctuary again.

"Sit still, will you?" Caroline said in a low voice. "You're making me nervous."

Jenna was nervous, as well, but she wasn't sure why. She wasn't the only one who waited anxiously for Dylan and Logan to show though. On the other side of Caroline, Mrs. Warren had an eye out for their arrival, too.

Some things never changed. Stories about Logan's and Dylan's late arrivals at church and the corresponding lectures from their mother went back as far as Jenna could remember. They lived so close to church that Mrs. Warren would make them walk if they weren't ready on time. Now they came from their own houses or apartments and still managed to be late.

Matthew had already asked the congregation to stand and turn to the hymn "O Holy Night" by the time the brothers slunk in, still wearing their coats. Their arrival was disruptive enough, but the two mothers made it more so by stepping into the aisle to let the two young men in first.

Jenna recognized the tactic to seat Dylan next to Caroline. Would those two ever give up? *Poor Dylan...er, poor Caroline,* she thought. Her sister wouldn't appreciate her lack of family loyalty. Caroline sighed next to her, a sound Dylan repeated as he opened his hymnal.

Jenna leaned forward to offer a waist-high wave to the latecomers, but only Logan waved back. Dylan sat with his gaze focused on the front of the church, his jaw flexing as if he was frustrated over his mother's matchmaking. Strange, as Jenna studied Dylan's profile, Haley's description of his "Greek statue–type cheekbones" popped into her head. She herself had never thought to describe him that way before, but now she could see why he could have been the subject for a sculpture.

Her cheeks burned at those odd thoughts. Even if she wondered why she'd never noticed before how handsome her friend was, she had no business recognizing it now…in church. She glanced around to see if she'd been caught watching him, but no one appeared to be paying attention. Relieved, she bowed her head for the opening prayer.

When next they were seated, Haley pulled her purse off the floor and started digging in its messy contents, probably for her offering envelope or a tissue for Lizzie. As Haley pulled her hand from the bag a few store receipts spilled onto Jenna's lap and another paper fell to the floor. Jenna handed the receipts back to her sister and then reached for the piece on the floor. She recognized the paper because she had one just like it. Only this one read "Dylan."

An idea popped into Jenna's head so quickly that she didn't have time to filter it before she leaned close to Haley's ear. "Hey, let's trade."

"Why?"

Reaching for her favorite designer bag, Jenna had no trouble locating her own slip of paper in an outside zipper compartment. She laid it on her sister's palm, and Haley unfolded it.

"Oh, I see," Haley said as she glanced down at her mother-in-law's name. "She's a tough one."

Haley had misunderstood her reason for wanting to switch, but Jenna couldn't bring herself to clear up the confusion. What was she supposed to say, that she was so desperate to be Dylan's friend again that she had to be the one to give him a gift? She couldn't explain to anyone else why it was so important when she wasn't sure herself.

She knew she'd felt more complete than she had for a long time just having the opportunity to be around Dylan. Something told her that her feelings hadn't always been so intense when they'd hung out together, but the difference had to be that she now realized how blessed she was to know him. At least that was the only explanation that made sense.

"Okay?" she said to Haley now.

"Fine."

They traded papers and then looked to the front of the church in time to see Matthew frowning at them from his seat on the podium. They were setting a bad example for Lizzie by whispering and passing notes in church. Jenna peeked around Haley to the child, but Lizzie was too focused on coloring in the *O*s on the bulletin to notice their bad behavior.

Jenna sat straighter, anyway, and grabbed her Bible as Reverend Boggs asked members to turn to the first chapter from the book of Matthew. Since her family and the Warrens had found a great service project to focus on over Christmas, she looked forward to an affirmation of that in the minister's Christmas message.

"Now Joseph was a decent man," the reverend began, choosing an unexpected character from the cast in the nativity story. "Even when he found out that the woman he was betrothed to was pregnant by someone else, he chose not to have her publicly shamed. Instead, he planned to divorce her privately and put the whole, unfortunate matter behind him.

"But God had other plans for Joseph, didn't He?" Reverend Boggs smiled down at the congregation. "God had tapped Joseph for the important task of being Baby Jesus' earthly father. In verse 20, an angel of the Lord appeared to Joseph in his dream, saying, 'Joseph, son of David, do not fear to take Mary your wife, for that which is conceived in her is of the Holy Spirit.'"

Reverend Boggs paused, allowing the congregation to ponder those words.

"Wouldn't it be great if God would send an angel to let *us* know His will for us?" he said, chuckling. "Or maybe He could reveal His presence to us in a burning bush like He did to Moses."

Several affirmative murmurs and a random "amen" rang out from around the room.

"For whatever reason, Our Father is subtler these days when He speaks to us. He does still speak to us, though. Never doubt that. We only have to listen."

Jenna glanced down at the biblical text again. She couldn't imagine how the minister had arrived at this message from the story of the nativity, but its unexpected twist spoke to her when maybe the traditional story wouldn't have. It convicted her, too, in a way she completely deserved.

Just like her split-second decision to force Dylan to work on a team with her had been about her needs, instead of his, her whole plan about reclaiming her friendship with him had been about what she wanted.

Not only had she never taken into account whether Dylan would even want to be her friend again, she'd also failed to consider God's will in the matter.

She might have become a new person when she'd turned her life over to God, but she still had the same selfish tendencies she'd always had. She'd wanted to be the one to work with Dylan, the one to make his gift.

Well, it couldn't be about her anymore. She could try to be Dylan's friend again but only because he deserved to have a good friend, not because she wanted it to be her. More than that, she needed to trust God to handle this and all the other situations in her life. She needed to concentrate on what God had to say. And, like Reverend Boggs had said, she only had to listen.

Early that afternoon Jenna watched with fascination as seven-year-old Connor Denton spooned the last bite of his caramel sundae into his mouth. She thought he might set a speed-eating record, but one glance across the ice cream parlor to where Dylan sat with Ryan shot down that idea. Connor's twin scraped the sides of his clear ice cream dish and might have licked it, too, if adults weren't watching.

"Aren't you cold?" She shivered at the thought of eating ice cream in December and curled her fingers around the coffee drink she'd ordered, instead. Even if there wasn't any real snow this week in Markston, it was cold enough for flurries.

"Not too cold for ice cream." The boy's teeth chattered a bit, though, and he pulled his new coat closed around his neck. The navy parka fit better than the one he'd worn the night they'd escaped from the fire, with its tight buttons and sleeves that didn't quite reach his mittens.

"Are you ready to work on your Christmas list? Your parents will probably be done soon at the coffee shop and will want to get you guys back to the hotel."

"Mommy and Daddy like to drink coffee for a long time, so they can talk about mushy stuff." The look on Connor's face suggested what he thought of such nonsense.

"Oh. I see."

Jenna's cheeks warmed as she peeked Dylan's way. She wondered if Ryan was telling private family matters over there, as well. Still, she was glad for the boys that even during this difficult time they never had to doubt that their parents loved each other.

Brad and Kelly probably wouldn't be in a hurry to force their rambunctious twins back into that hotel room, anyway. They'd already admitted to being stir-crazy after two days and had appeared relieved when Dylan had suggested that they go to the coffee shop next door, instead of joining them and the boys for ice cream.

"So, what would you like to put on your list?" She pulled the legal pad in front of her closer and poised her pen, waiting. "Do you want to write this, or do you want me to do it?"

"You can." He grinned. "My handwriting is messy."

"And we wouldn't want Santa to misunderstand your wish list, would we?"

"No way!"

"Okay." She looked down at the lined paper and wrote "Dear Santa" at the top. "What do you want to say?"

"'Dear Santa,'" he began to dictate. "'I know you'll

be busy with having to fly all over the world on Christmas Eve and stuff, but if you can find some time—'"

"Um," she said to interrupt him, "let's just start with the things you want, okay?" The peal of laughter coming from the other table suggested Dylan and Ryan were making no better progress than they were. She glanced down at the words she'd already written. "After 'some time,' why don't you say, 'could you please bring these things?'"

He nodded, tilting his head as if deep in thought. "For Daddy…some screwdrivers. Mommy would like…um…perfume. Stuff that smells like flowers. And Ryan likes building sets and puzzles. Oh, and comic books."

Jenna finished writing an abbreviated version of what Connor had just said and then looked at him, waiting. "And," she prompted when he didn't say more.

"That's all."

"What about for you?"

The boy drew his brows together as if he didn't understand what she was getting at. "I want them to be happy for Christmas. I want Mommy and Daddy not to have to worry anymore."

Jenna could only nod, thanks to the lump that had formed in her throat. Her eyes burned. Connor had lost his things in the fire, and when she'd expected him to ask for the mother lode of new toys, he'd thought only of his family. His selflessness humbled her. At seven years old, he'd already mastered the art of putting others' needs ahead of his own. She was still a novice.

"Can you sign it 'God bless you'?" Connor asked her. "Then I'll write my name, so Santa knows it's from me."

"Of course."

She looked away so the boy wouldn't see her blinking away the dampness in her eyes. At the same time, Dylan glanced up from the letter Ryan had been dictating to him, and their gazes connected. Dylan smiled and she felt her stomach drop out, close to what she felt during a plane landing but not quite the same. She expected him to look away as he had all the other times she'd caught him watching her with those evaluating eyes, but her heart must have beat a dozen times before he lowered his gaze to his notebook again.

If she didn't know better, she might have believed that smile was for her. More than likely, it was his response to some crazy gift Ryan had asked for, but she could dream, couldn't she? He hadn't smiled much since she'd returned to Markston—at least not at her.

She noticed how handsome Dylan was, especially when he smiled. It was as if that curve of his lips softened the hard lines of his jaw and chin, transforming granite to moldable clay. His eyes crinkled, too, perhaps the most appealing part of all. Shifting in her seat, her cheeks warm, Jenna looked back at her notebook.

At least he hadn't caught her studying him. That would have been humiliating. She glanced at Connor to see if he'd been watching, but the child was oblivious, his attention focused on her half-eaten strawberry sundae. As she slid it his way, his eyed brightened.

Probably before they wished to end their brief time alone, Brad and Kelly joined them in the ice-cream shop, and then Dylan and Jenna dropped the family off at their hotel.

"Now that was an odd experience," he said when they were alone.

"What do you mean? Going to the ice-cream place with just the boys?"

"No, that was fine. It was the stuff on Ryan's list." He looked away from her as he pulled his SUV into traffic.

"Does he want a laptop like Lizzie?"

The side of his mouth lifted at that. Matthew had confided to them about his daughter's grandiose Christmas list, but the child had only received a lecture on why greedy children ended up with empty stockings.

"Just the opposite. Ryan didn't ask for a single present for himself. Everything he asked for was for his mom, dad or his brother."

She turned sideways in her seat, the belt digging into her shoulder. "Connor, too. I even asked him if he wanted anything for himself, and he wouldn't budge."

"Neither would Ryan." Dylan cleared his throat.

"Well, they are twins," Jenna said. "If one of them asked for presents for his brother, he might be thinking he would get to play with them, too." Even as she said it, though, the words didn't ring true in her ears. "I don't think they had a scheme. That sounds more like something I would have done when I was a kid."

Dylan chuckled. "No, that isn't true. You would have asked for presents for yourself and then asked for some for Caroline and Haley."

"So I could play with all three sets."

"Never accused you of not being a smart child."

"You know me so well." She wanted to say he *used* to know her so well, but this was the best conversation they'd had since she arrived, and she didn't want to spoil it, even if that meant having to joke about the person she'd once been and hated remembering.

"I guess if we use Ryan's list, we'll know what Connor would like, and Connor's list will tell us about Ryan," Dylan said.

Jenna pulled out her notebook and looked at the letter she'd drafted. "And both boys told us things we could buy for their parents, though I wonder if every little boy thinks his mom needs perfume for Christmas and his dad needs screwdrivers."

"Ryan said perfume for Kelly and tools for Brad."

"Definitely twins." She chuckled and then became serious again. "Connor said he wanted his family to be happy for Christmas, and he didn't want his parents to have to worry anymore."

She waited for Dylan to share, but when he didn't say anything, she prompted, "Did Ryan say anything like that?"

He nodded as he cleared his throat again, focusing on adjusting his side mirror. Though he avoided looking her way, Jenna caught sight of his suspiciously shiny eyes. She had to smile at that. Dylan had always been tenderhearted—the protector of anthills, the secret fan of chick flicks.

He probably figured that sensitivity wasn't an attractive quality in a man, which was why he tried so hard to bury it. Jenna was surprised by how his lack of success pleased her. This was the Dylan she remembered. This was the friend she missed.

Though she'd been astonished when he'd taken charge of their adopt-a-family project, it had never surprised her that Dylan would have shown compassion for the family. Particularly those little boys. Whether he saw something of himself in them she didn't know, but she was grateful to Connor and Ryan, anyway. Not only had the boys shown her a great example of selfless love, they'd just given her a glimpse of her best friend, a man with a warm, compassionate heart. A man who didn't seem to be as lost to her, as she'd feared.

Chapter Six

"Now that wasn't so bad, was it?" Jenna glanced back at Dylan as they stopped near the exit of Sycamore Square Mall, their arms laden with shopping bags.

Dylan looked over his shoulder at the stores behind him with glass doors and metal bars already closed over their fronts. When he turned back to her, he wore a pained expression.

"Not as bad as losing a limb. But close."

"You're not overly dramatic or anything." She tried to shrug into her coat and balance several shopping bags at the same time, but finally she gave up and put her packages on the floor.

"Here." Already bundled, Dylan set his bags at his feet and helped her with her coat.

His fingers only barely grazed her shoulders before his hands fell away, and yet her skin tingled all the way down her arms. Startled, she looked back at the closed stores so he wouldn't notice her discomfort. She blamed the chill on the frosty breeze that sneaked through the door as the other shoppers exited. What else could it be? Giving herself a moment to collect her thoughts, she peeked into a few of her packages.

"You know my favorite part?" Dylan waited until she looked up before he continued. "The Sunday early-closing hours. They're great."

"Glad you liked them." She gave him a stern look, but she couldn't hold it.

Dylan swiped up his bags and as many of her bags as he could balance. "Okay, it wasn't as bad as I thought it would be."

Jenna had to agree with that. She'd been expecting the worst, or at least Dylan's worst griping, but he'd been pleasant. Helpful even.

"I couldn't believe how well you did with those store owners." She collected her few remaining packages. "Why did you think they would all be willing to donate something or throw in an extra discount?"

He pushed through the door and held it open for her. "I figured it wouldn't hurt to ask. The worst they could say was no."

"Well, none of them did." She shivered as she stepped out into the wind, wishing she'd zipped her coat before going outside.

"Did you notice I only approached store owners in the independently owned stores, instead of the chains?"

"I did notice that," she said.

"Managers from chain stores have to seek approval from corporate for donations, but local owners have the authority to make those decisions themselves."

"How do you know all that?"

"Mom has always forced us to work with her on charity projects."

Jenna hesitated, then decided to ask her question. "If your mom is so involved in charity, why was she reluctant when you suggested that we adopt the Dentons ourselves?"

He stopped next to his SUV and pulled open the hatch so they could put their packages inside. "She was just attached to her Christmas traditions and found it hard to let go of them. You know how that is."

"Sure." If she'd had some traditions, she might have been protective of them, too.

"Mom's just…I don't know."

She glanced at him, his strange words piquing her interest, but he stopped and lowered the hatch. He opened the passenger door for her and crossed to climb in the driver's side.

Jenna waited him for to resume the conversation, but he said nothing at all. She couldn't allow the silence to linger—they were finally talking again, and she didn't want that to stop.

"Well, anyway," she began, "I thought you were great today. I'm a good shopper, but you were an amazing negotiator. Because of the extra discounts you got the stores to give, we were able to buy more."

"You learn which store owners are easy marks…er, I mean the most generous souls. Seriously, though, remember, this is Markston. We take care of our own here."

Our own. How appealing that sounded, to be claimed as part of a community, to have a rightful place. Markston. Sure, she was born here and had lived here longer than anywhere else, but she didn't really belong anywhere. Her father had always called their moves "new adventures," but the shine had worn off early on. Jenna still wasn't convinced that the stress of his corporate climb hadn't led to his death from a heart attack.

"Whoa, what did I say?"

She peeked over to find Dylan watching her. He'd always been able to read her moods as if he'd had a personal invitation into her thoughts, so she shouldn't be surprised that it hadn't changed.

"Oh, I was just thinking."

"Must have been a sad thought. Want to talk about it?"

She wasn't sure she did, but she still found herself turning toward him. "My dad," she said finally.

"I thought it might be about him."

"How did you—" she started to ask, but then she stopped, lifting a shoulder and letting it drop. It probably wasn't that hard for him to guess what might make her sad. "It's still hard sometimes."

He nodded, pressing his lips together. "I should have attended the funeral."

"We understood. You had classes and clinicals. Your mom told us when she came. Your brothers couldn't get away, either."

"It was more than that for me, and you know it."

She shrugged because she did know. She also knew how hurt she'd been to receive just a customary flower arrangement when she'd desperately needed her friend's presence and support. "It doesn't matter," she said, because it was probably what he wanted to hear, but when he shook his head, she stopped.

"It does matter. I should have been there for you

no matter what…" He let his words trail away instead of rehashing the whole story. "Anyway, I'm sorry I didn't go."

"Thanks."

She didn't know what else to say, and because he flipped on the radio as they drove up Central Avenue on their way to her mother's house, she guessed he wouldn't be saying more about the past today, either.

"I guess I'll get started on my supersecret, home-made exchange gift tonight," she said when the silence stretched too long. She hoped she didn't sound too obvious. Now that she'd exchanged names to have his gift, she needed to come up with a good one.

"Oh, yeah. I have to do that, too." Dylan grabbed his forehead as though it suddenly ached. Then, glancing over at her, he said, "I'm not much of a craft guy."

She smiled. That was another thing she already knew about Dylan, but it didn't give her a hint about what to make for him.

Neither spoke again until Dylan pulled into her mother's driveway, and his question then showed he had other things on his mind besides gift exchanges.

"Did you notice Ryan and Connor squinting when we were at the ice-cream shop?"

"Well—" she paused, considering "—I guess Connor was a little when he was reading off the menu."

"Ryan, too. Could be a reading problem, but more likely myopia." He smiled at her raised brow. "You know, nearsightedness."

"Why didn't you just say that?"

"I wanted to impress you with my medical lingo. Are you impressed?"

"Very." She was surprised he would want to impress her. Surprised, and pleased.

"I'm having Brad and Kelly bring the boys in for eye exams tomorrow. I've convinced the senior partners to write off the exams, and then I'm going to talk them into giving the Dentons the glasses for free hopefully, as well."

"I'm sure they'll agree to it, too." She spoke without hesitation. She had no doubt that this new Dylan could convince the soldiers at Fort Knox to hand over the gold there for charity without anyone raising a weapon.

Dylan was confident in a way he had never been before. It was different, but Jenna liked it. Not *liked* it, not like that...but no matter how she tried to explain it away, she wasn't sure. She couldn't defend her reaction when he'd helped her put on her coat, either. Her chills might have to do with the company, not the weather. Could it be that this confident, charmingly persuasive Dylan was having an effect on her?

No, it wasn't possible. She couldn't be attracted to Dylan. He was like a brother to her. Right?

Right, she told herself.

He'd never been a clock-watcher. Dylan had always liked that about himself, so he hated admitting that he'd spent more time looking at the office clock that Monday before Christmas than he had performing eye exams. The only time he'd been focused all day was when Ryan and Connor took turns in his examination chair, and he was helping the boys to see clearly for the first time in a long time. But after that, he was back to watching the numbers change on the clock.

He was just itching to start work on the rental house

tonight. That had to be it, because he refused to believe he might be looking forward to seeing a certain someone after work today. That would be unacceptable.

As he drove to the Pearl Street house, he remained hopeful that Matthew had been exaggerating when he'd described the amount of work necessary to bring the rental up to livable standards. That was his perfectionist brother's opinion, and one man's hovel might be another man's castle.

He knocked on the door, and when no one answered, he pushed it open. His optimism sank the moment he got a good look inside, and he dropped the gym bag containing a change of clothes on a semiclean spot near the entry. Matthew hadn't exaggerated, after all. This place was a mess.

Eggplant-colored paint would have been an unfortunate choice for a living room in the best of circumstances, but here it appeared almost as if someone had thrown the color at the wall and carpet. The baseboards were split and falling off the wall, or missing entirely. But his observations were imprecise at best since the whole room was buried under an inch of grime.

"Oh, Dylan, you made it," Jenna said as he entered a bedroom at the end of the hall. She was crouched and scrubbing carpet no one should touch without a hazardous-materials suit.

She'd pulled her hair back in a ponytail again, and was dressed for hard work in faded jeans, an old sweatshirt and huge rubber gloves. As she scrubbed, her long side bangs fell forward over her eyes.

Dylan surprised himself by reaching his hand up as if to tuck the stray strands behind her ear, despite that fact that they were across the room from each other. Apparently that wasn't far enough.

Shoving his hand in the pocket of his khaki slacks, he gazed from side to side, searching for witnesses. Good thing no one else had been paying attention to him or he would have had to explain his tender impulses concerning his former best friend. He was having a tough enough time making sense of those himself.

But Jenna's sisters and his brothers were too busy to notice his strange reaction. They were peering up at a hole in the ceiling big enough for Lizzie to squeeze through. The rest of the room was covered in chipped, pea-green paint and filth.

Logan stepped over and slapped Dylan on the back. "We've got our work cut out for us, bro. Did you get a gander at the kitchen?"

"Do I want to look at the kitchen?"

"Depends," Logan said with a shrug. "As long as you don't want to cook anything, keep anything cold or wash your hands, it's a great kitchen."

"They took all the appliances and the kitchen sink?"

"They didn't want anyone to accuse them of taking everything but the kitchen sink."

Logan's joke earned moans from the others, but he seemed pleased with his comedy routine, anyway.

"It's going to be hard to wash out paintbrushes without a sink," Dylan said.

Matthew, still in his suit from work, grinned over at him. "Not to worry. Caroline and I are headed to the home-improvement store for a stainless-steel sink and some cleaners after I stop by the house to change."

"I hope you're picking up some paint, too."

"We thought we would start with cleaning tonight and then let you and Jenna pick up the paint tomorrow," Matthew said. "That way we can blame you if the colors look bad."

"Anything would be better than this." Dylan caught his brother examining the trousers and dress shirt he'd worn beneath his lab coat at the office. "I brought some clothes to change into."

"Good thing, because we're all going to get dirty," Matthew said.

"Lizzie's going to love that. Speaking of Lizzie, where is she? And where are Mom and Mrs. Scott?" Not that he was dying to meet up with the meddling moms and have Caroline shoved at him again. Caroline would probably catch a flight back to Chicago the day after Christmas, instead of waiting for New Year's, if they didn't stop soon.

Jenna stood up from her spot that didn't look any cleaner for her effort. "They're bringing back takeout." She paused, looking around. "I don't know where we'll eat it."

"In the cars?" he supplied.

"Either that or we'd better clean one good spot and make it into a dining room."

Dylan grinned and glanced at where she'd been scrubbing. "I don't think that one's going to be it."

Matthew and Caroline headed for the door to complete their errand, and Logan and Haley filed out of the room, searching for more damage like the "skylight." Dylan could only hope they didn't find anything to top that.

"We could rent one of those carpet cleaners from the

grocery store," Jenna said, though her frown suggested she wasn't convinced it would help.

Dylan shook his head. "We'll have to replace all the carpeting."

She looked at him over her shoulder. "Can we afford to do that? You might be an optometrist and Matthew might be a lawyer, but I fly in turbulent times in the airline industry. I'm not made of money."

"'Turbulent times'?" He chuckled. "Do you have any idea how much in student loans an optometry student can rack up?" Jenna shook her head. "I didn't, either. And Matthew probably won't pay off his law-school loans until Lizzie goes to college."

"Then how will we pay for carpeting, too?"

"Matthew said the owner was willing to split the costs for improvements, and if that's not enough, we can ask some other church members for donations. We should be fine, though, because I know a guy who owns a carpet store, and he'll—"

"Give you a deal, right?" She looked directly at him, her eyes narrowing. "You don't happen to know a guy who designs *haute couture*, do you?"

He studied her, grinning when he realized she was joking about her reputation as a clotheshorse. "Sorry. Can't help you out there."

She snapped her fingers. "Had to give it a shot," she said, and they both laughed.

Her laughter sounded like the tinkling of ice cubes in a tall glass of sweet tea. Before Jenna had come home, he'd forgotten how much he enjoyed hearing that sound, how easily it could touch a place inside him he'd declares off-limits. Now he was remembering exactly what it did to him and warning bells sounded in his head.

"We should replace the carpeting, then," she said. "We should make this place as special as we can for Connor and Ryan. Their biggest worries should be about which toys to play with, not whether they'll have a place to sleep tomorrow night."

"You really like them, don't you?"

"Can't help it. The boys, and Brad and Kelly. I can't imagine how hard it must be to worry about how you're going to provide for your kids. My heart just aches for them."

Dylan looked away, trying not to allow his surprise to show, but he knew he'd been caught.

"Why does it shock you every time I do or say something remotely decent?"

"I haven't been shocked," he protested, but when she looked back at him, her hands planted on her hips, he stopped. He didn't sound convincing, even to himself.

"People can change, you know. Even selfish, self-centered ones," she said.

"I know that."

"Do you?"

He shifted under her scrutiny. He didn't know why he continued to expect less of Jenna when she was proof that people could change. His mom had told him that Jenna had made a profession of faith a year or so ago, and everything he'd seen so far had confirmed a new, more benevolent spirit in her. She'd shown nothing but kindness to the Dentons, and she'd been nice to him, too, though he'd had a hard time being civil to her.

She had every right to her say now, so he waited, but she turned away, instead.

"Well, where do you want to start?" she asked.

Since he was bracing himself for an onslaught, it took him a few seconds to realize she was talking about the house, rather than the dressing-down he deserved.

"I'm sorry," he began, but she waved away his apology.

"Forget about it."

"Well—" he paused, looking around "—we could make a list of painting supplies and then start cleaning. I have a notebook in my bag." He started down the hall toward the bag by the door. "Later, we'll have Matthew get in touch with his landlord friend about the carpeting, so we can rip it out tonight. It'll be easier to paint without having to work around it."

"Will we have time to get it installed before Christmas?"

"Where there's a will, there's a way."

She nodded. In truth, he wasn't sure they would be able to get everything in place before Christmas no matter how much will they had. Dylan reached into his gym bag and grabbed a notebook and pen.

"We're really going to do this, aren't we?"

He smiled, allowing her contagious enthusiasm to push aside his worries. She'd told him to forget about the way he'd offended her, but amazingly, she appeared to have forgotten about it, as well. She forgave so easily, first about the funeral and now this. She didn't hold a grudge, either. As he changed in the one clean room of the house—the garage—he decided he should be more like her.

Now that was a thought he'd never expected to have about Jenna Scott, just as he never could have predicted that he would consider allowing himself to get close to her again. And yet, he was thinking about it.

Boundaries would be a must, of course, and he would never again be the human backhoe, waiting to scoop up the pieces after one of her failed relationships, but he could be some kind of…friend to her.

His confidence in that decision wavered the minute he stepped back into the house and headed for the rear bedroom. Jenna popped out of the closet where she'd been removing a broken rod and she nearly crashed into him. He reached out to steady her, and the feel of her arms nearly undid him. Suddenly his mouth was so dry that the house's lack of a kitchen sink became a personal affront. He simultaneously wanted to hold her forever and run from the room, never looking back.

Friendship with Jenna was impossible for him. It would never be enough. How many more times was he going to have to learn that lesson?

Chapter Seven

Jenna dipped her roller into a pan of butternut-colored paint and climbed onto the countertop to work. She wasn't skilled enough to use the painting pole without messing up the ceiling, so she had to make do. With Christmas only three days away, they were running out of time. Amateur painter or not, she was determined to do her part to finish the house so that the Dentons could spend Christmas in their new home.

Despite the amount of work they still had to do, Jenna was hopeful they would meet the tight deadline. Last night they'd installed the kitchen sink and then spent so many hours cleaning that she'd awoken this morning with stiff muscles. Dylan and Matthew had taken a few days off from work, and they'd all put in an eight-hour shift of painting with more to come.

Dylan had been able to convince the carpet dealer to not only offer a hefty discount but to schedule installation tomorrow. Now Matthew was waiting for a call from his friend at a freight company so they could have the appliances and furniture delivered by tomorrow afternoon. It could be done.

Careful not to drip paint, Jenna stood in a stooped position so she could roll the color along the strip of wall between the top of the cabinet and the ceiling.

"That works best if you put more paint on the wall, instead of on you."

At the sound of Dylan's voice behind her, she startled, bumping her head on the newly painted white ceiling. She glanced down at her sweatshirt, jeans and hands, all of which had been decorated with butternut smears.

"No comments from below, or you'll be up here."

"With you doing such a fine job? I wouldn't dream of interrupting genius like that." He stood, admiring the work for a few seconds before adding, "Hey, someone did a fine job of taping off the wall up there."

"I wonder who that could have been." She rolled her eyes at him.

Although he'd just turned down the job, Dylan snagged the painting pole Jenna had set aside, attached it to a new roller and started on a fresh section of the wall.

His reasons for working with her probably weren't what she would have hoped for—perhaps to cover up her painting mistakes or even to avoid being thrown together with her sister—but Jenna was pleased, anyway. For the first time since she'd returned to Markston, he was making the effort to spend time with her, instead of the other way around. And she found herself looking forward to every minute he was by her side.

At the sound of pounding feet, Jenna turned to see the Denton boys and Lizzie Warren bounding into the kitchen.

"Hi, Aunt Jenna." Lizzie tilted her head to the side to look up at her. "Look." She held out one of her braids, now tipped in the royal-blue paint from the boys' bedroom. "I have paint in my hair. Connor and Ryan have some, too."

"Mine has specks of blue, Mr. Dylan," Ryan said, pointing to a series of tiny blue dots.

"I have a blue ear." Connor also had a few blue fingers, which hinted at how his ear might have gotten its color.

"You all have a lot of paint on you, but the idea is to get most of your paint on the wall." She glanced at Dylan and found it hard to keep a straight face. "At least that's what I hear."

Haley hurried in with a damp cloth that she used to wipe some of the paint out of Lizzie's hair. She wiped the paint off the boys' hair and ears before whisking her stepdaughter from the room so Lizzie could "help" her parents in the living room.

"Boys, are you working in there?" Brad called out from the master bedroom where he and Kelly were painting the walls a sage green.

"Sounds like duty calling." Dylan stepped over to the small collection of unopened paint cans and selected a container of white cabinet paint. "If you guys help Mr. Logan clean up in your room, I'll teach you how to paint the baseboards with this stuff."

"Will you really? We get to really paint this time?"

Dylan nodded. "Really."

Ryan's eyes were wide with excitement, which could have been as much about the attention from their painting instructor as the opportunity to play with paint. Funny, Dylan seemed as excited as the boys were, though he'd already spent a whole day with brushes and rollers. His attachment to these boys couldn't have been more endearing. The twins probably weren't even aware how blessed they were to have a friend like Dylan. She'd enjoyed that blessing once herself and was beginning to think she might get to again.

"You two sure have done a nice job in here," Mrs. Warren announced as she and Jenna's mother joined the rest of them in kitchen. They rolled in the snack-filled cooler they'd brought over earlier to make up for the house's lack of a refrigerator.

"Almost done," Dylan said as he ran his roller sideways along the strip of wall.

"Well, then, Dylan." Amy cast a sidelong glance at Jenna's mother. "Don't you think that Caroline could use some help painting the hall bath?"

Jenna didn't have to look at Dylan to know that strong jaw of his had tightened. Her jaw was tight enough, and the moms weren't even meddling in her life. She could almost hear the matchmaking wheels cranking up again, and even the imagined sound of it grated on her nerves. Why couldn't they just leave Dylan alone? And, of course, Caroline. There had to be something she could do to help him avoid all this awkwardness. Uh, them.

"Have you ever known Caroline to need help with anything?" When several surprised glances turned Jenna's way, she rushed on, "I mean, she would never admit needing help, even if she did. You know, that whole she-is-woman-roaring thing, an ode to Helen Reddy."

Her gaze slid toward Dylan, and he coughed away what sounded like a laugh before looking back at his mother. "Anyway, I need to finish up in here."

"And then he's promised to teach the boys to paint moldings."

"He did," Ryan announced, his brother supporting his statement with an excited nod.

"Well, I suppose…" Trina Scott let her words trail off, her disappointment obvious.

The matchmakers excused themselves, probably to check in with Caroline and see if she really would refuse all assistance. They weren't going to win this one; Jenna could tell them that right now.

When the boys rushed off to help Logan so they would be ready to start on the baseboards, Jenna and Dylan were alone, and an unexpected awareness of that fact settled over her like static electricity. She couldn't decide whether she liked the sensation, only recognizing its newness.

"Thanks."

"You're welcome," she said without looking at him.

She didn't know for sure what his gratitude even meant—that he wasn't interested in her lovely sister, that their mothers' matchmaking attempts annoyed him, even maybe something completely different. When she finally worked up the courage to look at him, she found him watching her again, his eyebrows drawn together as if he couldn't quite figure her out.

"You go ahead and catch up with the boys. I can finish the rest of this and wash the brushes." She gestured toward the new stainless-steel sink that had already proved its usefulness as they'd all rinsed dozens of brushes, rollers and paint pans in it.

"You're sure?" He glanced up at the wall, unconvinced.

"I've watched you all day, so I know what I'm doing. I can handle it. Really."

He shrugged, then disconnected his roller from the paint pole, resting the roller on the pan. "Meet us in the garage when you're finished."

And then, before he left the room, he winked at her.

Jenna suddenly felt like a teenager again, just like when the captain of the football team had flirted with her. Dylan couldn't have been more different from that Neanderthal or any of the other boys she'd dated in high school and college, and yet she recognized those sweaty palms and the flutter of her pulse. She was not attracted to Dylan. She was just so happy that they were friendly again. That was all.

Dismissing any lingering doubts, she chose to focus on their earlier conversation, instead. She'd surprised him again by doing something nice, this time defending him. In all the years she'd known him, she'd never helped *him* with a problem. All the help and advice had always come her way. So it felt good to be the one watching *his* back. He needed a friend on his side to help him deal with the matchmakers, or he wouldn't stand a chance against their powers of persuasion.

But had she intervened for his benefit—or hers? She didn't want to ponder that because the answer might be as confusing as the electricity that had buzzed between them in the kitchen air. If this were anyone else, she would have read all that wattage as attraction, but this was Dylan, sweet, bookish Dylan, who'd always been more attached to his chemistry set than to any girl.

The new Dylan was different than the boy she remembered, but she still couldn't picture him with her independent older sister. Funny, she couldn't really picture him with any woman.

Except me.

As those words stole into her thoughts uninvited, her hand jerked, leaving a streak of butternut paint on the crisp white ceiling. Crouching down, she jumped off the counter and wet a paper towel before climbing up again. She didn't know where that thought had come from, but she shoved it to the back of her mind where it belonged.

Four years ago she'd messed up their friendship by not recognizing that his feelings for her had changed, and now that she had the possibility of restoring their friendship, she was trying to mess it up again by changing the rules. No, she would not let that happen. Too much was at stake.

Just as she touched the damp towel to the spot on the ceiling, Dylan pulled open the door between the kitchen and the garage and strode into the room.

"Well, there's an *oops*."

"I guess I didn't know what I was doing, after all." She frowned at the spot and started wiping, almost afraid to make eye contact with Dylan for fear he might smile at her and cause her to spill paint or something.

"Maybe you should blot at that, instead of wiping."

Dylan wet another sheet of paper towel, hopped up on the counter and started blotting. He was so close that their elbows bumped a few times and there didn't seem to be enough oxygen in the room for the both of them, but they quickly cleared away the mess.

He squinted as he studied the damp spot from a few

angles. "We might have to touch up the white a bit. Let's see how it dries."

All they needed today was something more to paint. "I just got distracted and…"

Dylan scanned the room, appearing to take in the plain wood cabinets, simple laminated floor and spaces where appliances would go eventually. "There's not a lot in here that could serve as a distraction."

Jenna could only smile at that as she avoided Dylan's gaze, hoping he wouldn't see the heightened color in her cheeks.

Dylan lowered the roller into the pan of white paint with a final-sounding *thunk*. They were finished. At least as finished as possible when the newly repaired ceiling in the second bedroom couldn't be painted for a few days. Still, they'd accomplished a lot today, painting all six rooms of the two-bedroom bungalow, plus a hallway. It was amazing what ten adults and three children could do with a short deadline and a lot of heart.

This was really going to happen. Brad, Kelly and the twins would wake up on Christmas morning in their new home, even if some of the smaller repairs would have to wait until after they'd moved in.

Dylan didn't know when it had become so critical to him that they meet this arbitrary deadline, when a few days either way wouldn't harm anyone, but it mattered. He wanted so much to return some small part of what the fire had taken from the Dentons.

"Are we going to nail the baseboards to the wall now, Mr. Dylan?" Connor asked as he rubbed his paint-covered hands together.

Dylan shook his head. "They need to dry longer." He didn't want to promise the boys they could help again when it was already late. That work probably would be completed after they were in their bed back at the hotel.

As if cued by his thoughts, Brad and Kelly pushed through the door into the garage. Dylan couldn't help but smile at the contrast between Kelly and Jenna after a day of work. While Kelly had only specks of green paint on her hands, Jenna wore an abstract painting of colors on her work clothes.

"Hey, you two, it's time for us to get back so you guys can go to bed." Kelly shook her head at her sons' automatic groans. "Now say good-night. We'll come back tomorrow."

While Brad corralled his boys, heading them inside to wash up at the sink, Kelly turned back to Dylan.

"I don't know how to thank you."

"You've already thanked us." He smiled. "Several times, actually."

She shrugged but grinned back at him. "I can't help it. This place is perfect."

"Perfect?" He lifted an eyebrow. "Did you see that drywall job Logan did on the ceiling in the boys' room? I wouldn't call *that* perfect. And the way the bathtub drips, I wouldn't call *that* perfect."

"You know what I mean. Your two families have been a blessing to us."

"Thanks." Dylan's throat tightened. The Dentons had been a far bigger blessing for him than he ever could have been for them. "So hopefully everything will come together, and you'll be home."

When the garage door opened again, he expected to see Brad and the boys, but Matthew came through first, flipping his cell phone closed as he approached. The rest of the workers tromped out after him, with Brad and the boys taking up the rear.

"I've just received word that we've hit a snag." Matthew sent an apologetic look toward Brad and Kelly before he continued, "The trucking company that was supposed to deliver the furniture and the new appliances couldn't schedule a delivery until next Tuesday."

"Isn't that December twenty-ninth?" Haley asked.

"Is that after Christmas?" Lizzie wanted to know.

Matthew answered both questions with a nod. "Apparently it's hard to get people to volunteer to work extra shifts right around Christmas."

For several long seconds, no one spoke. It was as if someone had let all the air out of a balloon. After riding four days on the drive of having a deadline, Dylan felt deflated.

"Aw, man," Logan answered for all of them.

Connor exchanged a sad look with his twin. "Does this mean we can't move in to the house?"

"You will, but just not yet," Dylan explained. "I know it's tough living in the hotel, but it will only be a few more days." Maybe he shouldn't make promises at all. He'd already gotten the boys' hopes up once, and look how well that had gone.

Ryan grimaced. "But what about Santa? We already left the letter at the old house, telling him we would be in this house. How will he find us now?"

"Now everyone," Jenna said, "let's calm down. This doesn't have to be a big setback." She turned to the boys. "We can go back to the site of the old house and leave a new note. I'm sure Santa will understand."

The boys nodded, looking relieved.

Jenna turned to Dylan. "You know, this isn't all bad. Sure, it would have been nice for everyone to be settled by Christmas Eve, but you said yourself that there were plenty of jobs still to do around here. The closets, for instance. Did anyone get around to painting them? And what about second coats? A few of the rooms could use them. And the moldings…" She lets her words trail away.

Several murmurs of consensus came behind Jenna.

"She does have a point," Brad said. He paused to glance first at his wife and then at his sons before continuing, "And, you know, this setback doesn't mean we can't sleep here on Christmas Eve, either."

He turned to Dylan. "Now, you said the carpet will definitely be installed tomorrow, right?"

"That's when they've scheduled it."

Brad gave a firm nod. "Then we're all set. We'll just bring sleeping bags…" He stopped, his gaze darting back to Dylan. "Do you have sleeping bags we could borrow?"

Dylan indicated his younger brother with a tilt of his head. "What do you say, Ranger Logan?"

Logan grinned. "Gotcha covered, buddy."

"Okay, then." Brad turned back to his sons. "We'll sleep in sleeping bags on the floor, so we can wake up on Christmas in our new house."

"You mean we get to go camping?" Ryan asked.

The room filled with hope again. Dylan had Jenna to thank for getting the process started. She hadn't let a minor setback discourage her, just as she hadn't let any of his off-putting behavior hinder her from trying to reconnect with him.

She'd become an amazing woman in the past four years—he couldn't deny it. She inspired and impressed him at every turn, and he felt…proud. Proud of who she'd become.

When she caught him staring at her, probably looking like a lovestruck teenager, he gave her a thumbs-up, hoping she couldn't read his mind.

Chapter Eight

Flipping on the overhead light in her mother's partially finished basement, Jenna jumped at the squeal coming from the far corner. Under only the illumination of a small desk lamp, Haley stood in front of an easel, a palette and brush in her hands.

"What are you doing down here?" Jenna asked as she padded from the carpeted area with its comfy couches to the section of bare concrete where Haley had set up.

"Shh. What are you trying to do, give away the location of my secret studio?" Haley waited until her sister stood next to her before she spoke again. "Mom said I could work down here on my secret gift."

"Your house wasn't good enough?" Jenna had claimed this place herself the other evening, and she was hoping to get some work done on Dylan's gift.

"Ever tried to keep a secret around a four-year-old?"

"Guess not," Jenna said.

"Matthew's no better. He keeps sniffing around the

house, looking for my gift. He's convinced himself I drew his name, and I figured I would just keep him guessing. That's why I told him I had to come work over here."

"Well, aren't you a sneaky one. Does Caroline know you're down here?"

"Sure, but she's been holed up in the guest room for hours working on her own gift."

Jenna stepped closer to the easel where her sister was putting the finishing touches on a painting of daisies in a vase. "Hey, that's amazing."

"I hope Amy will like it," Haley said. "Have you started on Dylan's present?"

"Kind of."

"Well, are you going to show it to me?"

Jenna lifted a shoulder. "I don't think so. It's not as amazing as yours is. You're the only one of us who's good at making crafts."

"I'm sure Dylan won't mind."

"Are you kidding? He'll probably laugh his head off when he sees it."

Haley was swirling a glob of white paint into a spot of yellow, creating a pale yellow color for some of her flower petals. "Why are you so worried about it, anyway? This is Dylan we're talking about. He'll like anything you make." She turned to study her sister. "Come to think of it, why did you need his name so badly in the exchange?"

Jenna noted that she hadn't fooled her sister with her interest in trading names, after all. "I don't know. It's just a friend thing."

"What's the deal with you two, anyway? You used

to be so close, and now there's a strange tension between you. It's almost as if—"

"Just a misunderstanding," Jenna said too quickly.

Haley lowered the cloth over her easel. "Well, Christmas is a good time for healing relationships. But then, at least according to the movies, it's also a good time for family brawls over the Christmas turkey."

Jenna frowned. "Thanks for the good thoughts."

"Don't mention it."

Finished for the evening, Haley set her palette aside and started up the stairs with her brushes in her hands. She stopped about halfway up and turned back to Jenna.

"Relax about the gift. And don't try to make it into a peace offering for your misunderstanding. Sometimes things take time to heal."

Haley pressed the fingertips on her free hand to her lips and blew a kiss. "See you tomorrow."

Once Haley had closed the door behind her, Jenna stepped to the row of metal shelves and pulled a shoebox out from a waist-high shelf. She carried the box over to the sofa and opened it. The scarf inside had uneven stitches, and some rows of gray and white were wider than others were, but she'd made it herself, and she couldn't help being a little proud of her effort.

Had she been making it as a peace offering as Haley had suggested? Was that the whole reason behind her need to have his name in the drawing? Or was it more than that?

Sitting back in the chair, she curled her feet under her and stretched the material across her lap. Then she pulled the crochet hook from the box, looped the yarn twice around it and slipped the second loop over the first.

She had better do a whole lot more looping, and fast, if she hoped to make Dylan's gift long enough to keep him warm this winter and have it finished in time for Christmas morning.

Glancing at the wall clock, she set to work on the first of several hundred stitches she would complete tonight. That would leave little room for sleep before tomorrow morning's cookie-baking event, but she didn't mind. She had a gift to finish. It would be a gift from her heart. No strings—of yarn or anything else—attached.

"Miss Jenna, look at this one."

Sitting on his knees at Mrs. Scott's kitchen table, Connor held up a spruce-shaped sugar cookie, so pitiful it could have been the inspiration for Charlie Brown's Christmas tree. Jenna applauded.

"My star is better," Ryan announced from his seat across from his brother.

The creation Ryan held in his palm had only four points instead of five, and it was sort of smashed in the center, so if anything, Dylan would have given the two cookies equal grades. Only they weren't grading.

"Do you like mine?" Lizzie held up an angel-shaped cookie that apparently had lost a wing.

"They're all wonderful." Jenna took a few seconds to ooh and ahh over each of the cookies before helping the children transport them from the flour-covered tabletop to the cookie sheet. "I'm sure they'll all taste great, too."

Kelly stood up from her chair to get a better look at the creations on the sheet. "Boy, you're all doing a great job."

"Those are some cookies, all right," Brad said with a chuckle.

Last night Jenna had invited the Dentons to join them for Christmas-cookie baking this morning, hoping to distract the boys from their disappointment that the house wouldn't be ready for Christmas. Dylan had been touched by her caring gesture and had also recognized the benefit of having the children out of the Pearl Street house while the carpet layers did their jobs, but he'd dreaded the idea when Jenna had first mentioned it. Just the thought of Christmas cookies had inspired memories of stress-filled holiday-baking events with their perfectionist pressure. At-home baking with a professional had its disadvantages. He'd been hoping to escape that family tradition when they'd adopted the Dentons for Christmas.

But so far, Jenna's cookie party had been more about the fun of creating than the products, more about time spent together. She didn't worry about cookies that only a child would eat, and she didn't even mind the flour in her hair or the food coloring that had splattered on her sweatshirt.

He was glad now he'd relented and invited his niece to join them, as well. This was the kind of memory he wanted Lizzie to have of Christmas.

At the beep of the oven timer, Jenna removed the first tray of cookies.

"Just look at these, everybody. Have you ever seen better cookies?"

"Well, not today…er, I mean, not in a long time." Dylan bit his lip and looked over at her, but Jenna only smiled. Come to think of it, he'd never seen Jenna bake before, and she'd never mentioned liking to spend time in the kitchen. He would have thought Haley had been the family's crowned baker, but it just went to show that he didn't know everything about the Scott sisters, after all.

"You never told me how you convinced our mothers not to attend this little shindig," he shouted over the buzz of the twirling beaters as she made frosting. "I'm surprised my mom didn't jump all over it and try to resurrect her Christmas-baking schedule."

"It wasn't easy. Your dear mother could convince a rottweiler to hand over his bone."

"Don't I know it."

"I had to rely on my own mother. I told her I planned to make a huge mess in her kitchen, and I was going to make her watch." She glanced over at him and shrugged. "She really hates messes."

"I remember."

"After I mentioned the mess, Mom was more than willing to convince your mother to go out with her for coffee, instead of joining us."

"Remind me never to stand in your way when you want something."

He leaned against the counter as the truth of his own words settled in. She'd wanted them to be friends again, and he was having a hard time denying her that. He no longer even wanted to. As he watched her, he expected her to gloat, but she wasn't looking his way. Only the slight upturn of her lips told him she'd even registered what he'd said.

Jenna placed the frosting, several butter knives and

a plate of cooled cookies on the table in front of Brad, Kelly and the three children.

"I'll be back in a minute," she said. "I have to go scrape some of this flour out of my hair."

As he watched her go, a familiar longing settled over him. He wanted to be with her, to be around her. But he tried to fight it. He'd already learned the hard way that to long for more than friendship from her was to swing out on a trapeze of faith with neither a safety net below nor any promise of someone to catch him when he fell. Only a fool would take a risk like that again. And he was no fool. What he'd been feeling for her these past few days was just…attraction. And he was strong enough to ignore that.

Shaking away those unproductive thoughts, Dylan glanced back to the table. Kelly must have taken Lizzie to the restroom while he and Jenna were talking because Brad was there alone with his sons, a new ball of dough on the table and a rolling pin in his hands.

The image was more a baking free-for-all than a sweet domestic scene, but no one seemed to mind. In fact, anyone who didn't already know about the tragedy this family had faced less than a week ago would never guess it from their happy faces. The boys hadn't lost everything; they still had everything that mattered.

It was the kind of simple, everyday, father-son moment that every boy deserved to enjoy, the type Dylan had no recollection of ever experiencing with his own father. But he wasn't jealous. He was pleased that the twins would have this kind of memory of their father, rather than an empty place at a table or an empty smile in a fading photograph. Like his.

Swallowing, he shook away unwelcome thoughts for the second time that morning. All these memories and feelings needed to stay in the past where they belonged. Was it Jenna's reappearance in his life that had stirred the sand of passing time once again? Or maybe it was just the holidays. Christmas could be the loneliest time of the year.

When he glanced at the kitchen doorway, he found Jenna standing there, her hair pulled back in a ponytail as usual. Only she wasn't watching the scene at the table. She was watching him.

When they were younger, Dylan had avoided sharing many of his feelings with Jenna even after his father had left and he really needed someone to listen. He'd worried that if his friendship became too cumbersome, she would pull away from the weight. But now as he read the warmth in her eyes, the compassion, he came to a surprising conclusion. She just might be one person—maybe the only one—who really understood. And that conclusion scared him more than even the realization that he was still attracted to her. Much more.

Chapter Nine

Amy Warren broke off a piece of blueberry scone, slathered it with butter and popped it in her mouth. She needed a sip of her Christmas-mint latte just to swallow it.

"Blueberry sawdust."

Trina grinned at her from across the tiny table at A Fine Cup coffee shop.

"Critiquing the baked goods again, Amy?"

"Why do you let me order things like this when we go out?" she said with a frown.

"A baker's standards are pretty high. That's why I talked you out of joining in on Jenna's baking party."

"Are you sure you weren't more worried about the mess?"

It was Trina's turn to frown. "I'll probably find flour in the crevices of my hardwood floors for months."

Amy spun her cup around. "But it would have been nice to get to share at least one of our Christmas traditions like we'd planned."

"Now, remember that I'm telling you this as your best friend who loves you. You need to quit pouting about the change in plans. You're being selfish, and I didn't even think you were capable of selfishness." Trina pinned her with her stare. "Our families are doing exactly what they should be this Christmas, trying to be God's hands in the world. That's how I raised my daughters, and that's how you raised your sons."

Amy swallowed as the truth of Trina's words struck her squarely in the heart. When she spoke again, she couldn't look at Trina's face. "I've always wanted the guys to be giving men. And they are. It's just that certain traditions are really hard to let go of."

"Especially the ones that helped us make it through the tough times," Trina added.

Amy nodded, though she wasn't ready to admit aloud that Trina was right. She acknowledged, though, that her friend understood her pain. Both had experienced devastating loss, although Trina's had been over losing her beloved husband to death while Amy's husband had deserted her and the boys.

"It's too bad we couldn't convince Caroline to host this activity with Dylan, instead of Jenna," Trina said.

Amy smiled, knowing her friend had purposely changed the subject.

"The Plan isn't working too well this time, is it?"

Trina shrugged. "It wasn't going swimmingly last spring, either, and we still ended up with our two families joined by marriage."

"It didn't turn out the way we planned, though," Amy pointed out. "If we'd had our way, Matthew would have ended up with Caroline, and then our two middle children would have paired off, followed by the youngest. But we were wrong."

"You yourself said that's because God has a sense of humor. Matthew and Caroline were too alike. But Caroline and Dylan? They're just different enough to be perfect together."

"Maybe too different," Amy said. "I just mean that Caroline is still sticking to her guns about this permanently single plan. She's got this idea that her lofty career aspirations are incompatible with marriage and family."

"Give her time. If anyone is patient, it's your Dylan. He doesn't kiss a lot of lady frogs while he's waiting for his frog princess."

Amy closed her eyes, shaking her head. "Oh, don't remind me." When her eyes popped open, she lifted an eyebrow. "That's quite a fairytale notion coming from a pragmatist like you."

"I was appealing to *your* romantic side."

"Have you considered that we could be wrong again?" Amy asked. "It is possible, isn't it?"

"Of course it isn't. What were you thinking? Caroline with Logan?"

Trina's incredulous tone told Amy what she thought of that. Amy had to agree. The man-about-town and the feminist? That would never happen.

"Or maybe you're thinking of Dylan with Jenna because they're the middle kids," Trina said.

"No, they were good friends for too long."

"So we have to focus on Dylan and Caroline, right?"

Amy nodded. And who knew? Maybe God really did intend Dylan for Caroline and would let all of them know eventually if they were only patient.

"It would be easier if they had an unlimited amount of time to be together."

"You don't think we should try another one of those ambush-date things, do you?" Amy winced even as she asked it. After their last dinner party, she was blessed that Matthew had ever spoken to her again. It had seemed like such a good idea to fly Caroline in and trick her and Matthew into having dinner together— that is until Matthew blew up and told both mothers to stay out of his love life. The only good thing that came out of that night was that it forced Matthew to admit he had feelings for Haley, instead.

Trina shook her head. "Caroline told me if I ever did something like that again, she would no longer consider me her mother."

Trina pressed her index finger to her lip, trying to come up with a plan. "Do you think either of them got the other's name in the gift exchange?"

"I don't know who has Dylan's name, but I know for sure that Lizzie pulled Caroline's name, since I'm helping her with the gift."

"We should have taken our names out so we could have known who everyone had."

Amy shook her index finger at her friend to indicate that was a great idea. "We'll do that next Christmas."

"We can't wait until next year. Biological clocks are ticking. We aren't getting younger, either."

"Speak for yourself," Amy said in a joke they'd shared many times as she was ten years older than her friend.

Trina pushed open the door, causing the attached bells to jangle. "I am speaking for me…and you."

Trina's lilting laugh mingled with the other Christmas sounds in Markston's downtown. "We have to find a way to get those two together in the next ten days."

"Ho. Ho. Ho. Merry— Hey, is anyone back there?"

The loud thud that followed surprised Jenna as much as the poor imitation of the jolly old elf coming from the living room. Wasn't Dylan supposed to be out running errands this afternoon?

"In here," she called, though she wasn't sure anyone heard her over the herd of buffalo that stampeded down the hall toward Dylan.

Before she'd made it to the living room, the scent told her what all the fuss was about: a Christmas tree. Dylan and Brad were wresting a huge plastic bag off its branches, but she could already tell it was more than big enough to fill the room's empty corner.

Sporting a Santa hat with his field jacket, jeans and boots, Dylan looked over the tree at her and grinned. He was thrilled with his gift, and she was excited for him. She'd been curious when she'd caught him watching Brad with the boys while they were baking. Did Dylan have any happy memories of his own father at Christmas like the ones she cherished, now that her father had passed on?

She must have stared too long because his eyebrow quirked. Disconcerting warmth spread over her neck and face, but she couldn't look away from him at first.

When she finally did, she reminded herself that this was Dylan, the friend of her heart, and she had no business looking at him like that. Even though she was tempted to look at him all day. *Unless...*

She didn't know how to process what was happening, but now wasn't the time. Soon. Sometime soon she would have to sit down and analyze these new feelings that scared her to death.

"Look, Miss Jenna, isn't it the most beautiful tree you've ever seen?"

From Ryan's wide eyes, she could see that he thought so. Having managed to take the bag off, the two men had set the tree in the corner. It brought some much needed color to the room, with its neutral walls and carpeting.

Jenna looked past Dylan to several items piled just inside the front door. Three new boxes of lights were laid next to another box with a star-shaped tree topper. Beyond those, two huge bags of popped popcorn were leaning against the wall.

Jenna cocked an eyebrow. "Hungry?"

"Popcorn garlands." He bent and picked up a small plastic shopping bag. Inside was a pack of extra-large sewing needles, scissors and two spools of heavy thread.

"You thought of everything."

"Not quite everything," Matthew reported as he entered from the kitchen, carrying a hammer and a short piece of molding for one of the closets. "Haley and Lizzie just went home for the shop vacuum. That popcorn's going to make a mess."

"Somebody always has to be the spoilsport," Dylan replied.

In her side vision, Jenna caught sight of Ryan and Connor trying to open one of the bags of popcorn.

"Wait!" Kelly called out, but she was a fraction of a second too late.

The bag split down the middle, and everyone watched as the boys fell away from each other, plastic and popped kernels trailing after them in opposite directions as they collapsed to the floor. Ryan and Connor scanned the mess and turned their guilty faces to their parents.

"See what I mean? We need a vacuum."

Matthew chuckled, and then the others joined him. The boys didn't seem to know what to make of it.

"Sorry," Connor murmured.

Ryan followed his brother. "Yeah. Sorry."

"Congratulations, boys. You've made it a white Christmas, after all," Jenna said.

"Yeah, look at this. You've made it snow."

Dylan exchanged a glance with her, his amazing eyes full of light and laughter. She quickly turned from him and went to the kitchen to find something they could use to clean up the popcorn. At least that was the reason she told herself as she fled the room.

An hour later they had formed several long popcorn garlands, and the boys were winding them around the tree to go along with the tree topper and strands of lights. When they were finished, they flipped off the ceiling lights and all stood back as Brad plugged in the Christmas-tree lights to a chorus of oohs and ahhs.

"It's so pretty," Kelly exclaimed. "Thank you so much for doing this, Dylan."

Though Dylan nodded and smiled, Jenna could tell that something wasn't right, so while the Dentons were preoccupied with the tree, she sidled over to him.

"What's the matter?"

He leaned close and whispered out of the side of his mouth, "The tree looks bare."

"Come on, Dylan. It looks great. And they love it."

He shook his head. "It's not finished."

Jenna studied the tree. She could see what he meant. Like the rest of the house, it looked incomplete. She scanned the room, looking for something they could use for decorations, but used paint cans didn't seem festive enough.

"I've got it." Dylan crossed the room to Haley, who'd returned with the shop vac just in time for cleanup. "Hey, do you think you guys can finish up here? I've got another errand to run."

"What do you have to do?" Jenna tried to keep the disappointment from her voice but knew she'd failed. She couldn't help it. Whatever this thing was between them, their days together were ticking away, and she wanted to spend as much time with him as she could.

Grabbing his coat from the pile by the door, he started out and then turned back to her. "You're coming, aren't you?"

Jenna grabbed her coat. She didn't bother to ask him where they were going. She didn't care. It didn't matter where they went as long as they could spend time together.

Chapter Ten

Dylan stuck his head inside the door, refusing to acknowledge any of the second-guessing going on in his thoughts. This was a good idea, and he wouldn't talk himself out of it.

"Mom? You home?"

"In here," Amy called from family room.

He slipped off his shoes and crossed into the room, waving for Jenna to follow. His mother was curled up on the sectional with a romance novel.

"I thought you might still be at the bakery." He walked to the couch and bent to kiss her cheek.

"Then why'd you come here?"

"I *hoped* you'd be here, silly."

Tucking a bookmark into the page, she lay her book aside and crossed her arms. "What is it, Dylan?"

He cleared his throat, hating that he was nervous. "We were just over at the Pearl Street house, which looks great with the new carpeting and the moldings." He cleared his throat a second time. "Anyway, there's a

Christmas tree at the house now. It's decorated with lights and popcorn garlands, but that's all. It looks kind of…"

Dylan let his words fall away as he turned to his mother's tree, its limbs drooping with the weight of their ornaments. He was still trying to come up with the right words when Jenna spoke up.

"It looks kind of plain," she told his mother. "Unfinished."

He turned back. "So I was hoping—*we* were hoping that you might be willing to donate a few decorations from your tree. I know they're special and all, but maybe you could spare some."

"It wouldn't have to be many," Jenna added, supporting his request, a request she'd known nothing about until that moment. "Just the ones without a lot of sentimental value."

He sent a grateful look her way, but when he shifted his gaze back to his mother, her bewildered face tore at his heart. She scanned the pieces of her overwhelming collection as if each held a special memory, and the memories were about to be stolen from her, one by one. Immediately, he was ready to backtrack. No charity project was worth making his mother this sad.

"You know, we don't have to—"

"Dylan." His mother spoke his name so softly that he almost missed it in his placating ramblings.

"Yes, Mom?"

She pressed her lips together for several seconds, and when she finally spoke, she didn't look his way. "Take whatever you need."

With that she walked out of the room, and soon her footfalls could be heard on the stairs.

"Why do I get the feeling there was a lot more to that conversation than the words you and your mom said out loud?" Jenna asked after a long pause.

"Because there was."

Though her curiosity all but thrummed in the room, she didn't ask. She deserved an explanation, Dylan decided, but that would have to come later, when the memories weren't so close around them.

He told her he needed a box from the garage, and when he returned, he found Jenna standing next to the tree, delicately touching ornament after ornament as if without knowing the whole story she understood the pieces' value.

She looked back at him over her shoulder. "These are all so beautiful. I never noticed before."

"It's hard to see any of them when they're all so crowded in there together."

"But that doesn't mean that they're not important to your mom. Are you sure we should be taking them? They all seem to have a lot of sentimental value to her."

"It's okay. Really." He nodded for emphasis because she looked skeptical. "Mom never would have agreed if she didn't mean it. She just left the room because it hurts too much to watch."

Jenna traced her finger over the miniature drum that was attached to a Little Drummer Boy ornament. "I don't know. Your mom seemed to be having a hard time giving up these things."

He pushed the box closer to the Christmas tree. "Some sacrifices are tougher than others."

He pulled off a little red sleigh and stuck it in the box. He didn't bother removing the green metal hook from it since it would be going back on a tree as soon as they returned to the rental house.

"Remember, we're taking from her abundance." He pulled off an animated pig dressed in Mrs. Claus getup and showed it to her. "I promise, we'll only take the ones with the least amount of sentimental value—none that my brothers or I made for Mom."

Jenna seemed to accept that and started removing a few items, showing them to him for approval before lowering them gently into the box. Soon they had enough ornaments to cover the Dentons' tree.

As he closed the top flaps of the box, Jenna turned back to the tree, folding her arms across her chest as she studied it. She glanced around the room at the other items blanketing the tables and windows. "Anything else you want to take?"

He stared at her incredulously.

"Joking," she said with a grin.

"I think we've traumatized Mom enough for one day. We can come back tomorrow and ask her to donate the giant plastic carolers in the front yard." He glanced toward the doorway and then leaned closer and lowered his voice conspiratorially. "I've always thought those old gals should carol some-where else."

"Well, Dylan Warren, you're not nice at all."

"You're just figuring that out now?"

"I'm a slow learner."

"Maybe, but when you do learn things, you master them so well that you could teach a class." He hadn't meant for his comment to sound so serious, but as soon as he said it, the truth in his words struck him.

She *had* learned a lot of things, and he'd become the one who needed to be taught.

Jenna blinked, but she didn't comment on what he'd said.

They gathered the box and their coats. Dylan paused at the bottom of the stairs to call up to his mother, thanking her and telling her goodbye.

"I'll call her later tonight," he said to Jenna when his mother didn't answer.

The only sounds during the drive from his mother's house to the rental house were the whir of the engine and the carols coming from the all-Christmas-format radio station.

He was trying to come up with a way to broach the subject when she turned just as he put the car in park. On one of the shortest days of the year, darkness had already settled, so they couldn't see each other, but he could still feel her gaze on him.

"Tell me something, Dylan."

"What's that?" He shut off the engine and turned to face her.

"What's the real deal with your family and Christmas?"

Until Dylan started laughing, Jenna was worried that she'd brought up a topic that was even more off-limits than she'd guessed. But he'd invited her into this story when he'd asked her to come along to his mom's house, and she couldn't help being curious.

"You sure know how to phrase a question," he said as his laugh tapered off. "My family and Christmas. Let's just say that Hollywood doesn't make warm Christmas specials about Warren-family Christmases."

He seemed to be waiting for her to contradict him, but she'd seen enough now to know that all had not been perfect over the Warren-family holidays. She settled with her back against the car door and waited for him to fill in the blanks. She might know some of this already if she'd only been listening years ago, but there was nothing she could do about that. She was listening now, and now was what mattered.

"Christmas was always a frantic holiday at our house, long before my…father left."

The catch in his voice made Jenna long to reach out to touch him, but she wasn't sure how that gesture would be received, so she clasped her hands in her lap. "Why do you think that is?" she prompted when his pause lingered.

"Mom was always making up for the fact that Dad— my father was never involved in any of it. He never came to our Christmas pageants at church, never had time to look at our Christmas lists. He would show up to watch us open presents, but he always had the TV on."

She didn't miss that Dylan was uncomfortable referring to Elliot Warren as Dad. He had every right to his anger at the man who'd deserted his family. She was furious on Dylan's behalf.

"Your dad sounds so different from the man I knew when our families went on vacations together," she said. "He seemed pleasant."

Dylan shrugged. "He was different at home. Mom must have believed that if she filled every holiday minute with frantic, festive activities, my brothers and I wouldn't notice he was missing. So each year she added more activities, and the holiday seemed more desolate."

"That must have been strange," she said, "feeling lonely and alone in a frenzy of activity and people."

He nodded. "The Christmas celebration was just a symbol of bigger problems."

"You know how jealous I used to be of all your family Christmas traditions?" she said, shaking her head. "As often as we moved, we barely had any traditions at all. You guys had all these amazing events, and I wanted that."

"That coveting thing is in the Ten Commandments, you know. Thou shalt not covet they neighbor's house. Thou shalt not covet thy neighbor's Christmas celebrations," he said in a solemn voice. He tried to keep a straight face, but then he started chuckling. Jenna couldn't help laughing with him.

"We're even, then, because I used to envy *your* family," Dylan said.

"You're serious? Even with all the moves? How could anyone envy that?"

"You took everything important with you each time you moved."

Jenna considered that for a moment. Dylan was right. Even without a permanent landing site, she and her sisters had always enjoyed support from two parents who loved them. Not everyone had been so blessed.

"I never thought of it that way," she said. "I didn't think about a lot of things back then."

"The narcissism of youth."

"Or just mine."

He didn't disagree with her, but she hadn't expected him to, either.

"Why didn't you tell me the truth about your family back then? We talked all the time, but I don't think you ever told me any of it."

"How could I? You had to think I was strange enough already. Being a chemistry-set nerd was bad enough without the sad home life." He lifted a shoulder and let it fall. "I didn't want your pity."

"I wouldn't have pitied you." But even as she said it, she wasn't so sure. The truth was, she didn't know how she would have reacted. She hoped she would have been supportive. "But I told *you* everything. Probably more than you wanted to know."

"I always wanted to know," he said in a quiet voice. Then he straightened in his seat as if his admission had surprised even him.

Jenna didn't know what to make of that confession, but the rest already had made her feel terrible. He'd always been there for her, but she'd failed him again and again. She had to fight the urge to reach over and pull him into a hug. "I'm sorry, Dylan."

"For what?"

"For not being the kind of friend you needed and deserved. I wish I'd been the type of person who put others ahead of herself, but I wasn't."

He cleared his throat a couple of times as if he had something momentous to say. When he finally spoke, though, it was only to dismiss her apology. "It doesn't matter. It was a long time ago."

She wanted to tell him that it did, but he opened his door and climbed out. He went around the back of the

SUV and opened the hatch. "We'd better get this stuff inside. We can finally finish decorating the tree."

She didn't want their conversation to end. He'd opened up to her in a way he never had before, and it seemed like he was about to share more. But she had to be satisfied with what he'd told her. Maybe he'd decided she was worthy of his trust again. The thought of it made her as excited as the boys were about the tree. It was happening. She was winning him back.

"All finished," Dylan called out as he hung the final snowflake ornament on the Dentons' tree. "Doesn't it look great, guys?"

"It's cool!" Ryan exclaimed.

"Yeah, cool!" Connor agreed.

All the adults, minus Dylan's mother and Mrs. Scott, had gathered back at the Pearl Street house again. They stood admiring the tree, its pine aroma competing with the smells of fresh paint and new carpeting.

Dylan turned to Jenna. "You see, *now* it's finished."

Jenna smiled, and his chest filled with warmth. He'd been surprised by how much the activity of hanging the ornaments with Jenna, the twins and Lizzie had affected him. Or maybe he was still reeling from his intense conversation with Jenna.

With his history of sharing little with her about his life, he'd found it surprisingly easy to open up to her now. But what he'd been tempted to say to her affected him more than anything he'd actually said could have. When she'd told him she wished she could have been a more magnanimous person, he'd wanted to assure her that she was that kind of person now.

Sharing that with her wouldn't have been so bad if it hadn't felt so intrinsically tied to another admission he would be forced to make to himself. Despite his best efforts at keeping her at a distance, his old feelings for her were back in full force, and there was nothing he could do about it. What happened to his promise that he would never let her get under his skin again? Didn't he ever learn?

"Hey, I recognize some of these."

Logan's words brought Dylan back from the journey of his thoughts. He was relieved that no one seemed to notice that he'd been daydreaming.

Logan took a cherub-shaped plastic ornament in his palm. "Aren't these things from—"

Dylan cut him off with a quick shake of his head.

Logan's gaze darted between his brothers. "Oh, yeah. This stuff looks great." He turned to Brad and Kelly and their boys. "You have a great tree to go with your great new home."

"It's so beautiful. You're all so wonderful." Kelly's eyes were shining as brightly as the Christmas lights.

Brad walked over to his wife and draped an arm over her shoulders. "She's right. You've outdone yourselves. You didn't have to do any of this, but we're so grateful." His gaze flitted to the tree and back. "Where did you get all this stuff?"

"From my mother's tree," Dylan admitted.

Matthew shook his index finger at the tree. "I thought I'd seen some of it before."

Dylan held his hands wide. "They're gifts from my mother."

Dylan didn't miss the raised eyebrows from both his

brothers, but that would be a discussion for another time. In fact, for a long time, he and his brothers had needed to have a little Christmas conversation with their mother. Until now, they'd all been reluctant to broach the topic, but things had changed today. He'd opened a door by asking her to donate part of her ornament collection, and his conversation with Jenna had convinced him it was time to talk to her.

Thinking about that discussion would be better than dwelling on his feelings for Jenna. He needed to step away from her, to find some perspective, but that was awfully hard when they were working together.

He was on dangerous ground, and he knew it. At first, he'd just been struck by her beauty, but that was nothing new. Now, every time he saw her, he found something else to admire about her, from her kindness to her humor to her warmth. Even knowing it would be foolish to allow himself to fall for her again, he found himself standing on the edge of the cliff, waiting for the courage—or madness—to leap.

But, he quickly realized, he was forgetting something important. He shouldn't assume reality had changed just because Jenna had. There was one truth that could keep his feet rooted in place, no matter what was happening to his heart. For whatever reason, he wasn't the guy she wanted. He never had been, and he probably never would be.

He would do well to remember that.

Chapter Eleven

Something had changed between them. Jenna was convinced of it, even though he had agreed to her suggestion that they stop for coffee when they left the rental house. Dylan was across the table from her, sipping a cup of dark roast, but he seemed thousands of miles away and probably would have been if he didn't have to drive her home. Last week she hadn't minded him spending time with her out of obligation, but now she wished he'd chosen to be near her, instead.

That wasn't likely to happen. He'd been acting oddly around her ever since the conversation in the car earlier. It couldn't have been clearer that he was sorry he'd shared details about his past with her. If only she'd minded her own business, instead of nosing into his life, asking about his family's Christmas celebration.

Why couldn't she just let him keep his secrets and his pride? But she couldn't let it go any more than she'd been able to let him keep his distance. She might have known him all her life, but she realized today that she'd never really known him at all.

He'd been her steady rock in the choppy waters of adolescence, but he'd never allowed her to see that he, too, had been scared and lonely. She wanted to see now. She wanted to know him, to know what made him tick, what made him happy or even still scared him, though the last he tried to hide.

"Hey, I wanted to thank you for listening earlier," Dylan said.

Jenna looked up from her latte. "Thank me? I thought you would never forgive me."

"That, too." He paused and grinned at her over the top of his cup. "But you got me thinking and talking about something I've needed to discuss with my mom for a long time now."

"Why do I get the feeling I've just messed up the delicate balance of noncommunication that has worked so well in the Warren family? The whole clan will probably collapse in a heap."

He shook his head as he set his cup aside. "We're a family of guys. What can I say? Noncommunication works well for us. Well, most of the time. It's families of women that have to beat every subject to death."

She raised her hand,. "Guilty. But our family won't die of heart attacks over bottling up our feelings, either."

"None of us have." He shrugged. "Yet."

He turned his head to glance at the coffee shop's display of baked goods.

"Hey, those cherry turnovers look good. Want one? My treat?"

Jenna smiled at his obvious attempt to change the

subject, but at least he didn't suggest they take their coffee to go.

"Are you sure your mom won't be hurt that we're eating treats from the competition?"

"To spare her feelings, we'll keep it between us, okay?" he said with a wink. "Besides, she wouldn't want us to starve to death, would she?"

"Of course not," she said, continuing with the joke.

But as she waited for Dylan at the table, she suddenly felt even more flustered than when she'd first returned to Markston. Her nervousness was different this time, though, as if they were on a first date or something. It was a silly daydream, of course, but part of her wished that dream were real.

"I should have known that all this would come up when we took on this project," he said as he sat down and handed her a plate with a turnover on it.

"What would come up?" she asked, certain he couldn't be continuing the conversation about his family.

"All this…*stuff.*" His said the word as if it was something distasteful.

"You mean about your dad?" After his nod, she took a deep breath and decided to forge ahead. "I can see why the Dentons' situation would have hit a little close to home for you. You connected with Ryan and Connor right away, and it was easy to see why you did."

His expression was guarded, but still he asked, "Why do you say that?"

"A pair of little lost boys? You could relate to them because you used to be one of them even if their loss was different from yours." As soon as she said it, Jenna braced herself, certain she'd gone too far. How could she presume to know anything about sad little boys or their losses?

"When did you get so smart?"

"Are you kidding? I've always been brilliant." Although she played down his praise, her cheeks warmed with pleasure. "You just never noticed."

Dylan stared at her, the look in his chocolate eyes so intense that Jenna forgot to breathe. His gaze—so warm, so true—made it clear that she was wrong. She could say a lot of things about Dylan but never that he'd failed to notice her. *She* was the one who hadn't been paying attention.

Chewing her bottom lip, she lowered her gaze. When she glanced back at him again, he was staring out the window. She had so many questions about Dylan now. His thoughts, his feelings and his dreams— she suddenly needed to know all of those things.

"I saw you this morning when you were watching Brad with the boys," she began, choosing just one of her questions. If he didn't want to talk about it, she was sure he would let her know.

But he only nodded. "Ryan and Connor seemed to love his attention."

"I couldn't help wondering what was going through your mind. Were you thinking of your dad? Do you have memories of good times like that with him?"

He shook his head, giving her the answer she expected.

"But I wasn't thinking about that when I watched them," he said. "I don't dwell on stuff like that." He took a sip of his coffee. "It wouldn't fit with my rugged, manly persona."

She smiled but didn't say more because she suspected he was working up to a real answer. Finally, he spoke again.

"I was happy when I watched them," he said. "Happy for Brad and Kelly, too. The Dentons will weather this difficult time because they have each other. That's the most important thing, and a lot of people don't have that."

A lump formed in Jenna's throat. Dylan had missed out on a lot of things in his childhood, and yet he'd still learned to value what really mattered. "I couldn't help thinking about my own dad when I watched Brad with the boys," she told him. "My sisters and I had plenty of war stories from when Dad tried to get us to work together in the kitchen."

She stopped and smiled, the memory warming her now, instead of creating that familiar ache inside. "That includes the time we invited the fire department over to put the fire out in the oven."

"Sounds like a great time to me."

Jenna was suddenly aware that her hands rested so close to his on the table that if she moved her fingers the tiniest bit, they would be touching. She swallowed as she realized how much she would like that. No, she couldn't keep having thoughts like this. Couldn't let herself be attracted to Dylan. Unfortunately the force that pulled her to him was becoming harder to resist.

Her cheeks burning, Jenna gathered her courage and looked up from the table. As she expected, Dylan was studying her.

"You really miss him, don't you?"

Jenna blinked. She hated that he'd misunderstood

the reason she'd become quiet and that she couldn't tell him the real reason, but what he'd said was true, as well.

"Yes, I miss him." Her eyes burned, but somehow, she managed to keep her voice from shaking. "It's worse on holidays."

He nodded, a sad smile resting on his lips, and she ached inside to think how well he understood.

"I told you I used to be jealous of your family sometimes, but it was mostly about your dad."

Of course, he would have longed for what he'd never known. She, on the other hand, had been blessed to have such an amazing father, but she'd taken that blessing and so many others for granted while she'd mourned the lack of permanency in her life. She'd forgotten what really mattered while she was longing for a permanent home.

"My father was an amazing blessing. When he passed away last year, it was the lowest point of my life." She glanced at Dylan and found him looking at her in a way that made her long again to reach for his hand. "When I flew into Indianapolis, Haley met my flight to tell me Dad had died."

"I can't imagine how hard that was for you."

"Your dad is still living, isn't he?"

"As far as I know," Dylan replied. "No one's called us to claim a body or pay off any debts." He closed his eyes, shaking his head. "Sorry."

"Don't be sorry. You have every right to be angry. Your father's desertion totally changed your life, and Matthew's and Logan's."

His eyes opened, but he braced his hands on the edge of the table and leaned back in his chair, staring at his coffee, instead of looking at her. He seemed to weigh her words, deciding if he could agree with what she'd said.

"So...would I have been a different man if my father hadn't left?"

He seemed to be talking to himself as much as to her, but Jenna heard the pain and the uncertainty in his question. The need to reassure him overwhelmed her. She couldn't let him go on thinking he was somehow less than the amazing person he was.

"You might have been a different man," she acknowledged, though she hated agreeing with even that part of what he'd said. He needed someone to ease his doubts, and she wanted to be the one to do it. "But there's no way you could ever convince me that you would have been a *better* man."

Jenna reached over and clasped her hand over his, unable to hold back any longer. It was an act of comfort, of support, and that was all, she told herself. When the strong, firm hand stiffened under her touch, she realized her mistake. Dylan would never want her to see him as weak, as in need of her nurturing. She'd worked so hard to move closer to him these past few days, and in a few seconds, she'd just negated all of that effort.

When she looked up at him, Dylan was staring at their hands in surprise or confusion or some other emotion. He swallowed visibly and didn't speak for so long that Jenna was convinced that whatever he said next would be something she didn't want to hear.

"Thanks," he said finally.

Her sigh of relief had almost escaped her lungs when Dylan turned his hand under hers and laced their fingers together. She drew in a sharp breath. As much as she tried to tell herself that he'd only accepted her gesture of comfort, the strumming tingle that extended from her palm all the way up her arm made the excuse sound flimsy. And though they were in the middle of a coffee shop, she felt as if they were the only two people in the world at that moment, connected in a way that seemed so right.

Giving her hand a squeeze, Dylan unlaced his fingers from hers. "Shall we go?" he asked, standing up.

Jenna's fingers continued to thrum as she put on her coat. She felt strangely empty without the feel of his hand in hers.

Neither of them spoke during the ride back to Jenna's house. Dylan didn't know how he could with the complex conversation already going on inside his head. But the silence only seemed to add to the electric charge between them.

They'd shared too many thoughts and words and emotions for one day. As for him, those words and feelings dug through so many layers of his history that he ached from the excavation.

He didn't know what to make of his willingness to open up to her, let alone that touch they'd shared, which had about as much to do with simple compassion as his mother's holiday-village collection had to do with Christmas.

Okay, Jenna might have reached out to *him* in solace, but the moment her fingers had rested on his hand, he could think of nothing besides her soft skin and her warm touch. His lacing their fingers together had seemed like the most natural thing in the world.

"Did you hear me, Dylan?"

He startled as her words drew him back to the present. He'd just pulled to the curb in front of Jenna's mom's house, so he waited until he'd turned off the engine before he turned back to her. She was watching him in the illumination that filtered in from the streetlight.

"No. Sorry. I wasn't listening."

"I wanted to ask you a question."

Swallowing, he nodded and waited for the expected question. How could he tell her what he'd meant by the whole hand-holding incident when he wasn't sure himself?

"Why did you really end our friendship?" She must have read his surprise because she rushed to explain, "I mean, it had to be more than just that one misunderstanding over my canceling on you, right?"

He shook his head. She still didn't get it. "It wasn't just a misunderstanding."

"I know it wasn't. I mean, I should have gotten it that you thought our date was…well, a real date. And even if I didn't get that, I knew we had plans, and I shouldn't have canceled just because I had…"

"A better offer," he supplied.

"No, that wasn't it," she began, but she stopped herself.

"It was a long time ago. Let's just forget about it."

"I don't want to forget," she said. "I want to know."

"Fine," he said on a sigh. The truth. He'd spent so many years hiding it and then even more trying to forget about it. But she deserved to know, even if it was years too late.

"I was always crazy about you, even when you were eleven and crying over your new braces."

The look of surprise on her face only made him smile. "It started there, but it only became stronger over time. Through every one of your boyfriends and heartbreaks, I was there waiting for you to recognize that I had feelings for you. But you never did."

"Why didn't you ever tell me?" she said in a quiet voice.

"I guess I was afraid of losing the little part of you I did have. The part that belonged to the best friend alone."

"But you changed your mind." If possible, her voice sounded even smaller this time.

"Even everymen reach their limits eventually. You know, like George Bailey in *It's a Wonderful Life*."

"Only you would bring up that movie," she said, chuckling. "You were never an everyman."

"Anyway, when you canceled our date that you didn't even realize *was* a date, that was the last straw for me. I had to do something for myself, and that meant I had to make a clean break."

"So you couldn't be my friend anymore."

The sadness in her voice touched his heart. "Like I said, it was a long time ago."

"That doesn't make it right. I totally disregarded your feelings and made you feel as if you were unimportant. It was wrong, and I'm so sorry about it."

He nodded. They both stared out the front windshield, lost in their thoughts.

"What does all that mean for us now?" Jenna asked finally.

"That doesn't—"

She rushed on, not allowing him to finish, as if she couldn't bear to hear the answer to her question. "I mean, I came here hoping that I could make things right with you. I'll do whatever it takes, but I want you to know that I don't want to give up on us."

"Are you going to let me speak?" A smile pulled on his lips.

"Oh. Sorry." She took a deep breath.

"You've been trying to apologize to me ever since you got here. A long time before that, even. It was wrong of me not to forgive you. Besides being downright un-Christian. So, I forgive you, and I'm sorry." He shifted in his seat, uncomfortable with apologies. "I was hoping that you would, you know, forgive *me*." He shrugged. "You know that whole 'forgiveness is divine' thing."

"You're asking *me?*"

"I guess I am."

"Then I forgive you."

"You make that sound so easy," he said with a chuckle.

"It is when you're feeling blessed to have the chance to appear so charitable." She paused, clearing her throat, and when she spoke again, her light tone had disappeared. "It's just that, Dylan, I can't picture my life without you in it."

He took a deep breath, trying to slow his racing heart. They'd just moved beyond apologies and forgiveness to something less easily defined. He couldn't afford to let himself read anything into her words, though. Yes, she wanted him in her life, but she'd always wanted that. Nothing had changed. It would be dangerous for him to think so.

Still, she sat beside him, so vulnerable, so unsure. He couldn't leave her dangling that way, wondering what he thought about her admission, wondering if he cared at all. He owed her the truth, no matter what it cost him.

Tightening his hands on the steering wheel, he let the words come. "I can't imagine my life without you, either, Jenna."

Chapter Twelve

Dylan sat at the same desk where he'd beaten his head against his calculus textbook on more occasions than he cared to recall. Now he was banging his head for another reason entirely. So he'd drawn Jenna's name. Big deal. He didn't know why he was making it so complicated. Yet Christmas Eve was tomorrow, and he still wasn't sure what gift he would give Jenna on Christmas Day. Or rather…which.

What happened to his thinking he'd received a raw deal when he'd pulled her name in the first place? When had it become so important to him that his gift to her be the right one?

Probably when they'd held hands. Or admitted they wanted to be in each other's lives.

He glanced down at the papers spread out on the desk in front of him. One of them was covered with so much ink that the words on it were almost indecipherable. Another, the one with the ideas on it, had most of its lines crossed out. Settling his elbows on the wood, scarred with the dents and glass rings from the irresponsible teenager who'd once worked there, he looked at the other option, which he'd set in the corner of the room.

Either the birdhouse he'd made as a kid or the gift on the desk would fit the letter of rule if not the intent, as Matthew would say in his legalese. Both were definitely homemade; only the time frame of the creations could be called into question. The birdhouse was almost finished, but the other gift? He could finish the other one if he put his mind to it…and sacrificed his pride.

Was he ready to do that? Was he ready to put himself out there and take a chance at falling flat again? He shook his head. Where was his sense of self-preservation? His answer to her question about why he'd put her out of his life made him wonder. But what did he have left to protect when he'd already told her the truth about the past? Only that he'd never really gotten over her, but he refused to give away that little detail.

He tucked the sheet of blotched paper in the top desk drawer to let the ideas stew again. From the corner of the room, he collected the birdhouse and opened a small can of paint he would use to finish and update it. The pungent smell made his eyes water, but it at least helped him to think of something besides the piece of paper in the drawer. It was an imperfect structure, all right, with its less-than-square walls and tiny door that had shown his amateur skills with the jigsaw. But it might have to do.

There was still time to choose between the two gifts. As much as thirty-four hours, if he pushed it. But he would have to decide eventually, and then he would have to live with the fallout from the choice he made.

* * *

Jenna pulled her coat higher about her throat as she and Dylan trudged through downtown Markston, searching for last-minute gifts for the Dentons. With the fifteen-degree temperature drop they'd experienced since last night, it felt more like shopping farther north in downtown Detroit, instead of southern Indiana. Maybe there was a chance for Christmas flurries after all.

Instead of festive, the air about them felt frantic as shoppers bustled from store to store, all under the pressure of finding the perfect gift before Christmas Eve early closing hour. Jenna's disquiet had nothing to do with the remaining shopping hours, and Dylan's restlessness mirrored hers. Clearly their conversation from the night before had confused him as much as it had her.

"Well, what's left?" Dylan rubbed his hands together to produce heat.

Jenna gestured with a nod toward his hands. "Forget your gloves?"

"In the car." He stuffed his hands in his pockets.

She pointed down the street. "Just the specialty toy store and the candle shop."

"Good. We need to get this over with."

Jenna gave him a sidelong glance as she trudged down Washington Street. Somehow she didn't think his comment had anything to do with shopping. When they reached The Toy Maker, Dylan opened the door for her and then disappeared into the back of the store to browse.

She supposed she couldn't blame him. If he felt even half as vulnerable as she did, she could understand his need to put some space between them. Not that his reprieve would be long. Even after they

finished shopping today, they still had Christmas Eve
services ahead tonight and the family gathering
tomorrow for Christmas Day.

Jenna wished for a little space herself, yet she
realized that would do as much good as wishing she
hadn't asked him last night why he'd walked away
from her years ago. Last night, she'd needed to hear
what he would say, but as soon as she'd asked, she'd
known the answer. The truth was that in her heart,
she'd always known how Dylan felt about her when
they were younger. She'd just chosen *not* to know it.
How could she reconcile herself with that? Sometimes
the extent of her selfishness back then still shocked her.

She'd known Dylan her whole life, so it was strange
to feel as if she was seeing him now for the first time.
This strong, honest and amazing man had been there
right in front of her, and the only way she could have
missed seeing him was to have lived her life with her
eyes closed. Maybe she had.

She stood before a floor-to-ceiling display of
puzzles, barely seeing any of their colorful boxes as
she caught sight of Dylan farther down the aisle. He'd
squeezed his lanky frame into a junior-size chair at a
display table featuring some sort of industrial-style
building set, and he was manning the mechanical
controls. He was too focused on the task to even notice
her gaze or how she smiled as she watched him.

The inquisitive boy she'd always known was still
there, the boy who'd put grapes in the microwave just
to see the sparks and who'd performed an experiment
with toilet-bowl cleaner that had nearly caused an
explosion.

Of course, she'd always cared about Dylan. She'd been drawn to her friend in the same way that an injured individual is connected to the crutch that helps him make his way in the world. But this Dylan—the man—pulled her to him in a way the boy never had.

Now, her gaze followed the contours of his beautiful, strong jaw, and those firm lips pressed into a straight line of concentration. The long fingers of his hands were curved around the controls. She now knew how safe and warm his hand could make a woman feel when he laced his fingers through hers. How safe and warm it had made *her* feel.

Jenna blinked, not sure what to do with all the thoughts and emotions clamoring inside her head, each vying for top position.

He said he'd always been crazy about her. Was that a past-tense *always,* or did he still feel that way? If he did, would she have the courage do anything about it?

What was she thinking? Dylan was an amazing man; there was no denying that. He was as gorgeous on the inside as he was handsome on the outside. No wonder she couldn't help feeling drawn to him as any woman with good sense would be.

But it wasn't good sense for her. She'd waited so long for Dylan to give her a second chance, and he'd amazed her by finally forgiving her. Whether they would ever be the kind of friends they'd been in the past, no one could predict, but one way to guarantee they wouldn't get there would be to allow herself to become attracted to him.

As tempting as it was to follow these new and different feelings, she couldn't afford to take the risk.

Relationships failed, even more often than marriages, and she knew the statistics on those. If she and Dylan were to begin a relationship, and that relationship were to fail, she would lose their friendship, too. How could she bear to lose him again?

The truth was she couldn't bear it.

She shot another glance Dylan's way and this time found him grinning at her. He gestured with his hand for her to come over to see something, childlike excitement in his eyes.

No, she couldn't risk their friendship again for anything, even some silly daydream that they could be something more than friends. She shook her head to strengthen her resolve and walked over to Dylan.

When she reached the display table, he pointed down at it. "I think Santa should get the boys one of these."

"One of these?" She leaned over the contraption, trying to cover the flush in her cheeks from her earlier thoughts.

The toy was fancy, all right, with its motorized cranes and pulley systems, as well as its trucks and train cars waiting to be filled from huge piles of coal and logs. It wasn't what she would have pictured, but she admitted she'd struggled when they'd been shopping for Ryan and Connor. Although they'd already found some puzzles and comic books, nothing else at the regular toy store at the mall had seemed like a good fit.

"You're sure about this?"

"Oh, yeah. I would have given my eye teeth for something like this when I was their age."

She narrowed her gaze when she looked his way. "Are we shopping for the twins or you?"

"Them, of course. They love to build things. They like to see how things work together and come apart."

"And you know what a boy like that would like because you used to *be* that boy, right?"

He answered with a grin.

"Well, did you find the box anywhere? It is Christmas Eve, after all." Jenna glanced around, and then she saw it. Only one box remained, just to the right of the display table. She pulled it out so she could look at the price, and when she did, she gasped. "Dylan, did you see this?"

She pointed to the two-hundred-dollar price tag, which was more than a toy had any business costing. "This is too expensive."

"But it's perfect," he said simply.

"We don't have this much left in the budget." In fact, their working budget was stretched about as thin as it could be without popping any holes.

"Can't you find something else that the boys would love just as much?" she asked when he didn't answer. "They won't mind. Remember their Christmas lists?" She hoped that by reminding Dylan about their wish lists, he would rethink the plan, but he wouldn't budge.

"Come on, Dylan. Brad and Kelly would never have been able to buy this for their sons, even before Brad's job loss. Even before the fire." She paused, trying to plan her words just right. "We can't buy happiness and security for them no matter how much we'd like to."

She expected him to bristle under the criticism of his motives, but he wouldn't budge. "That's not what I'm doing. Their family gives them all the happiness and security they need. This is only a gift, the kind that encourages them to stretch their minds to see possibilities rather than roadblocks. It reinforces the stuff their parents are already teaching."

Though she couldn't argue with his reasoning, they still didn't have the money to pay for this gift, and they couldn't approach any of the other church members for funds to purchase an extravagant toy. She would have told him that, too, if he hadn't yanked out his wallet and pulled out a stack of twenties.

When he caught her watching him counting the money, he tapped President Andrew Jackson's face on the top bill. "I've been saving up for a new snowmobile." He paused and then shrugged. "It'll be a while longer."

He would probably be waiting a lot longer, Jenna guessed, since this wasn't the first rogue purchase he'd made this week. When the senior partners at his optometry practice offered him a discount on the boys' eyeglasses, instead of the *free* eyeglasses he'd hoped for, he'd covered the rest of the bill himself. Jenna's mother had bound her to secrecy over that bit of information.

It wasn't until Dylan carried the huge box to the cash register and plunked his money down that Jenna realized what had just taken place.

"You'd already picked this thing out for the boys, hadn't you?" She pointed to the box. "You knew how much it cost, and you already had the cash on you."

"Whatever do you mean?" he asked, his lips twitching.

She looked around the store with suspicion. "How often do you come to this place to play—I mean, demonstrate use of the toys?"

He assumed a thoughtful pose, gripping his chin between his thumb and forefinger. "Hmm. Before this week, maybe once or twice a year. You know, gifts for my niece."

"But as busy as we've been this week, you still found time to get over here by yourself and pick this out?"

"Errands, remember?"

She nodded, smiling. "But you hate shopping."

He shrugged as he smiled back at her. Would Dylan ever stop surprising her?

She hoped he never did.

As he came to his feet, taking his place next to Logan among the basses, Dylan looked to the conductor and winked, though he doubted Matthew could see him clearly in the low lights and candle glow. Dylan had to give Matthew credit for pulling together a melodic-sounding choir from this crew of mediocre voices, Dylan's own superior in its mediocrity.

From his place in the back row of singers, he scanned the middle and front rows, his mother and Mrs. Scott joining Haley in the soprano section, while Jenna and Caroline stood side by side in the alto section. His mother positively sparkled as she took in the herd of Warrens and Scotts, all corralled in the choir loft to sing in the Christmas choir.

As the opening strains of "Silent Night" filled the sanctuary, Dylan grinned out at their guests, the Dentons, who were sitting in the second row. It only seemed right that Brad and Kelly and the boys would join them for Christmas Eve service after the week they'd all spent together. Lizzie, who'd insisted on sitting between Ryan and Connor, waved up at her family.

Dylan was happy for his mother that she'd had the

chance to share another of their family's Christmas traditions with the Scotts, but he was even more pleased for all of them that it had been this particular custom. This one had been special to him once upon a time.

For reasons he didn't bother trying to explain away anymore, he shot a glance at the person who had also been special to him back then and who had remained in his heart no matter how hard he'd tried to extricate her from it. While the rest of her family appeared to be caught up in the serene spirit in the sanctuary, Jenna seemed edgy, as if she could feel his gaze on her and would have wished it away if she could have.

That same uneasiness had seemed to cling to her the whole time they'd been shopping together. Several times at the toy store he'd caught her watching him with what he thought was pity. During those moments, part of him wished he'd said nothing about why he'd pulled away from her. But only part.

Sure, he hated feeling this vulnerable now that the words were out there between them, instead of tucked safely in his thoughts, but at the time he hadn't been able to stop the words from coming. Just once, he needed her to know what had been inside his heart, even if he regretted telling her later.

He also could have told her that those feelings hadn't ebbed over time, but he wasn't ready to do that any more than he was ready to ban her from his life again. He didn't know how she felt, anyway. Sometimes he sensed something between them, but that could have been wishful thinking. He'd proved years ago that he wasn't above reading too much into simple friendship.

Because none of the questions inside him could be settled tonight, Dylan pushed the thoughts away and focused on the words Reverend Boggs spoke in the opening prayer. Like the others around him, he settled in his choir-loft seat and pulled his Bible from beneath the pew.

He didn't want to go through the motions as he had so often in the past few years. Tonight he wanted to fully experience the service, to absorb the sight of the manger scene in the corner, the scents of pine and candle wax and the sounds of familiar carols and scriptures. More than any of those things, though, he wanted to feel God's sweet spirit, which Reverend Boggs described in his prayer.

Tonight, Dylan listened with rapt attention to the verses in the second chapter of Luke, some of which he could quote by heart. The story sounded so real to him, such truth in the arrival of light for a dark world.

"'And suddenly there was with the angel a multitude of the heavenly host praising God, and saying, "Glory to God in the highest, and on earth peace, good will towards men."'"

As Reverend Boggs had closed the passage at verse 14 and invited the congregation into a moment of contemplation, Dylan couldn't help looking over at Jenna. From behind her, he could see only her profile as her head was bowed in prayer. He couldn't begin to explain now why he'd allowed the fiasco between them four years ago to cause him to lose his way with God.

He hadn't blamed God for not giving him the woman he'd wanted; it wasn't as simple as that. He'd just lived his faith on autopilot, just as he had some other elements of his life. It was the lowest point in his life, and he'd turned his back on his faith, just when he'd needed God's comfort most.

Again he looked at Jenna as she continued her silent prayer. What a contrast there'd been between the way they'd faced their darkest days. While she'd reached out to God in her time of need, he'd turned away from Him, instead. He didn't have to ask himself which of them had found more peace. That was obvious in the serenity on her face.

A smile pulled at his lips as he lowered his head and began a silent prayer of his own. He'd never expected to learn life lessons, let alone faith lessons, from Jenna Scott.

Father, you know I often take the longest path to reach You. Thanks for waiting around for me until I do.

When he looked up again, Jenna was smiling at him. She mouthed the words that would mean more to him this holiday season than ever before. "Merry Christmas."

Chapter Thirteen

"Merry Christmas, dear one." Mrs. Warren crossed the family room, gathered Jenna's mother into her arms and kissed her cheek.

"And Merry Christmas to you." Trina returned her friend's kiss.

Amy was the last to join the crowd, as she'd been finishing up in the kitchen, so they'd all dispatched with coats and pleasantries before she arrived. That just meant another round of hugs and kisses was in order before they could get to the presents that seemed to be occupying Lizzie's attention.

"When are Ryan and Connor going to get here?" Lizzie asked.

"Soon," Matthew told his daughter. "The boys are opening their gifts from Santa at their new house first and coming here for Christmas dinner."

"We'll *never* get to open presents, then." Her voice became a whine.

"Never open them?" Dylan nabbed his niece and

swung her around in a circle. "I heard you already opened a bunch of presents from Santa at your house this morning."

Her sour expression immediately disappeared. "I got a bike and two dolls." She pointed to the two curly-haired baby dolls propped up on the mantel.

"Those are really nice. Since you've already had presents, I guess you won't need the one under the tree," Dylan joked with his niece.

"But these presents are special because we made them," she told him.

Those wrapped gifts beneath the tree were special, all right. Jenna was only uncertain about one of them: the one she'd made for Dylan. She'd been pleased with the scarf when she'd finished it last night, but now it seemed woefully inadequate, especially when compared to Haley's painting.

Mrs. Warren practically floated over to the Christmas tree, her holiday spirit back in place. Jenna was impressed with the tree itself, its branches less weighed down now.

"Since the rest of our guests weren't involved in the gift exchange, I don't see any reason why we can't open the gifts now," Mrs. Warren said.

Or we could wait, Jenna wanted to say, but since Lizzie was already jumping up and down and Dylan's mom might as well have been, she didn't bother. Her gift would have to be enough.

Most of them gathered on the sectional and side chairs, and Logan sprawled on the carpet near the fire so that Lizzie could distribute the gifts, with reading help from Haley. The child lowered a box, about twelve inches square, at Jenna's feet. Jenna was more curious about what Dylan would think of the gift in the small red box in his lap than she was about her own gift.

"Who do you think should go first?" Matthew asked.

His daughter raised her hand. "Me, Daddy. Me. Me."

"I don't know, pipsqueak." Logan shook his head. "What do you guys think?"

"Logan Michael Warren," Mrs. Warren said.

Dylan learned over and thwacked his brother on the back. "Whoa, brother, it's not even noon yet on Christmas morning, and you've already earned the three-name threat. You should pace yourself."

Lizzie did get to open her gift first—a sweet rag doll Trina had made—and then the others took turns clockwise around the room.

Jenna held her breath as Dylan pulled the tag off his gift and read the name on the back.

"It's from Jenna." He smiled her way and then pulled the red wrapping from the box. Lifting off the lid, he brushed his hand on the gray-and-white-striped scarf Jenna had crocheted. "Hey, this is great. Thanks."

He pulled the scarf from the box and wrapped it around his neck, preening for their families. Jenna knew he was just being kind—it was the most average crocheting job anyone had ever done—but he made her feel as if she'd just given him the most amazing gift in the world.

As he started to set the box aside, he noticed the other item she'd put in there. He pulled out the card and read it silently. When he'd finished, he met her gaze and nodded. "Thanks again."

"What does it say?" Haley wanted to know.

Dylan brushed away the question with a wave of his hand. "It's just a Christmas card."

And it was. The card wasn't even homemade. The handwritten message inside it was part of the gift, though, and she was relieved he'd chosen not to share her words: *I wanted to return some of the warmth you have always given to me.*

As Dylan tucked the card back in the box and tossed his wad of wrapping paper in the garbage bag Caroline had brought from the kitchen, Jenna finally was able to relax. He not only had liked her gift, he had appreciated the feelings that were tied in with each stitch.

By the time most of them had opened their gifts, Jenna was really enjoying herself. The gifts were as varied in content as they were in craft quality, but each recipient accepted them with the love with which they were made. Caroline fussed over the pair of colorful pot holders Lizzie had made on a child's loom, and Haley couldn't stop complimenting Logan on the tiny pine Christmas tree he'd whittled for her from the small section of trunk he'd cut from the bottom of his mother's Christmas tree.

"Okay, it's your turn, Jenna," Trina told her daughter.

Jenna lifted her box off the floor and glanced down at the card. She flipped over the tag and read aloud the name that made her pulse quicken. Dylan. "It's from Dylan."

"You're the only two who got each other's names," Logan pointed out.

The look her mother exchanged with Mrs. Warren left little doubt that the two of them would have preferred someone else to share the tradeoff with Dylan.

Jenna decided not to reveal that she had orchestrated hers and hoped that Haley wouldn't give her away.

"Aren't you going to open it, Aunt Jenna?" Lizzie asked.

Jenna took a deep breath, trying to look as casual as she could. She was probably putting too much importance on something as simple as a gift exchange, but she couldn't help wondering if Dylan would make a statement with his gift the way she had.

"Of course, I am Lizzie. I love presents."

"Remember, Jenna, this one won't be a designer fashion," Matthew joked. "It's from Dylan Warren, not Calvin Klein."

Frowning his way, Jenna pulled the gift wrap from the box. "I'm sure I'll love it whatever it is."

Fighting her temptation to rush, she removed all the paper before untaping the end of the box.

Jenna could only hope that no one read her reaction when she saw what was inside, because it shamed her. She wanted to be able to appreciate the gift just because he had chosen it for her, but she was having a hard time understanding the gift. The birdhouse he had built when he was a boy? Still, she tried her best to be gracious.

"Thanks, Dylan."

Reaching into the box, Jenna pulled out a red-and-green-painted structure. From its scent, she could tell he'd given it a fresh coat of paint. He'd also personalized the gift with the words, "Jenna's House," which was the only thing personal about it.

"It's great," she added, and she made herself meet his gaze and smile. She tried not to let herself think that a birdhouse was something to be put up at a home, the thing she still didn't have after all these years.

"Hey, isn't that the thing you made when we were kids?" Logan asked.

"The only rule was that the project had to be handmade." Dylan told him. "Not that it had to be made this week."

Logan grinned. "Way to take the easy way out."

"Now, Logan," Mrs. Warren began, "you know how busy Dylan's been this week. And he's right. We didn't say the gift had to be made recently. Just homemade."

She scooted over to Jenna's side and examined the house further. "It was a nice touch to personalize it."

"Thanks, Mom." Dylan, who had crossed the room to stand behind his mother, leaned down to buss her check. "Now go open your present. You're the last one."

As his mother returned to her seat to open her present, Dylan stayed where he was, next to Jenna.

"I hope you're not too disappointed," he said in a low voice.

"Why would I—"

"It's not a handmade scarf." He tugged on the tasseled end of the one still encircling his neck.

"I love it. Really." The more she thought about it, the more she did like it. He'd taken a piece of his past and remade it for her. Maybe there was something personal in that, after all.

Dylan shifted next to Jenna, drawing her attention away from Mrs. Warren and the painting she was gushing over. Jenna lifted an eyebrow and waited for him to explain.

"It's just that I had to choose between two gifts,"

he said with a shrug. "So I chose the one with Christmas colors."

If only he'd turned away then, Jenna would have accepted his explanation without question. He didn't. He continued to look at her, his lips pressed together as if he wanted to say more.

Jenna could barely restrain herself from grabbing him by his navy sweater and insisting that he say whatever he'd held back. She was still considering doing that when the doorbell rang, announcing the Dentons' arrival.

Brad and Kelly and their boys paired through the door, Ryan and Connor lugging the box for their building set with them. When the boys immediately found a corner and pulled Lizzie along so they could set up their toy, Jenna exchanged a secret smile with Dylan. He'd been right about this special Santa gift.

The adults returned to the Christmas tree to let Brad and Kelly open a few gifts. One turned out to be a gift from Mrs. Warren alone: a crèche from her collection. But the hit turned out to be the date-night package, which included a gift certificate for dinner, movie passes and free babysitting from Dylan and Jenna.

Once those gifts were opened, Matthew slipped out of the room, and soon the prelude from "Away in a Manger" filtered in from the piano in the living room.

Taking her rag doll with her, instead of the two fancy dolls she'd brought from home, Lizzie skipped out of the room to join her dad at the piano. One by one, the adults and children set aside their gifts and followed the musical sound. Singing voices soon blended with the piano.

Now Dylan and Jenna were alone in the family room. He gestured for her to precede him, but as she stepped next to him, she glanced at him. The intense look in his eyes stole her breath away. Straightening, she took another step, but he reached out a hand to rest on her sweater-covered upper arm.

"Merry Christmas, Jenna."

With her heart pounding so hard and the skin on her arm tingling beneath his touch, she struggled to find her voice. "Merry…Christmas, Dylan."

He squeezed her arm and then pulled his hand away, leaving a warm and prickly place where his touch had been. "We'd better get in there. We have the whole family holiday celebration ahead of us today."

She nodded, unsure whether she could trust her voice not to give away her disquiet if she spoke. She'd never been so nervous around Dylan before. Or so agitated. Or so thrilled. She couldn't begin to know what to do with any of those jumbled feelings.

Motioning for her to follow, Dylan started out the door into the hallway that separated the family room from the living room, but Jenna barely had enough time to catch her breath before he glanced back at her.

"It's going to be a great day," he told her. "But soon…"

That he let his words trail away like that made her crazy. She waited for him to fill in the blank, but when he didn't, she couldn't help prompting. "Soon?"

He gave her another meaningful look that made all her nerve endings spring to life.

"Sometime soon, after all this is over, you and I need to talk."

* * *

The long table in his mother's dining room was more cramped than Dylan could ever remember, and food on the platters was disappearing at a rate alarming enough to rule out the possibility of leftovers. But neither of those things dampened Dylan's spirits as he looked along the table that he shared with his family and friends, and Jenna. She looked more beautiful today than he could ever remember. He was nervous about the conversation, but the time had come. Words needed to be said. At least, *he* had to say them.

His mother held court at the head of the table, smiling at her collection of guests, accepting compliments about her legendary Christmas dinner with grace.

As Dylan smiled back at her, the realization struck him that this was his favorite Christmas ever. It didn't matter that the week had been even more hectic than any of his mother's regular Christmas extravaganzas. It didn't even bother him that he was sore from painting and tired of shopping and even that he and Caroline were seated next to each other again. Out of necessity, they'd become adept at ignoring each other in close proximity.

Spending the holiday giving back to others was part of what had made this Christmas special for him. A large part. But he wouldn't lie to himself by saying that was the only thing that had made this holiday extraordinary. He attributed the rest to Jenna.

Automatically his hand went to his neck. It felt bare without the scarf around it, but he would have had a hard time explaining why he had kept his scarf on when even Lizzie had left her rag doll on the mantel with her two new plastic friends. Still, he couldn't get over the thoughtfulness of Jenna's gift. Her lovely, imperfect scarf only made his substitute gift seem more inadequate.

"This dinner is amazing, Mrs. Warren." Brad indicated the turkey and ham and trimmings of the traditional Christmas dinner, plus the Warren family standards of pierogi, kielbasa and cabbage rolls. "Thank you for including us in your family Christmas."

"We're just pleased you could be with us," she said with a smile.

"I don't know how you managed to get everything done with all the time you all spent helping…" Brad let his words trail away, his voice thick with emotion.

Amy Warren waved away his comment with a brush of her hand. "There were plenty of us, and many—"

"—hands make light work," several other voices finished for her.

"Well, it's true," she'd said with feigned annoyance.

Before anyone had the chance to say more, his mother clapped her hands. "It's time for dessert."

"I wonder what it will be." Logan tapped his lip a few times before guessing. "Cake, maybe?"

"Of course, cake," she said, rolling her eyes at her youngest son. "What you should be asking is what *kind* of cake." Her enthusiasm building, she stood up from her seat and waited.

"Okay, I'll bite," Matthew said. "What kind of cake do you have for us, Mom?"

Seated next to Brad and Kelly, Dylan leaned over to explain. "I don't know whether we mentioned this or not, but our mother owns a cake shop."

"This is the *kind* of cake we have today." Amy slipped through the door and returned with a rolling cart and a cake that would have been perfect for a party of one hundred, rather than just thirteen. The three-tier cake was white like Christmas in Markston hadn't been, and it was covered with green piping that looked like garland and red flowers shaped like poinsettias. Like a wedding cake, this confection had a topper, but it was a miniature manger scene, and next to that was a birthday greeting for the Christ child.

"Wow, Mom, you've really outdone yourself this time. I don't even know how you hid this thing," Dylan said.

"I still keep a few secrets up my sleeve." Amy crossed her arms over her chest, appearing pleased with herself.

Dylan felt the resentment of Christmases past disappearing. All his mother had ever wanted was to make her celebrations a fantasy for the children in her life, and today she had mesmerized the three children with her king-size gesture.

"I think Mrs. Warren deserves a round of applause for this one, don't you?" Dylan clapped, and the others joined him.

As his mom handed out pieces of cake, Logan sampled the vanilla mousse filling, closing his eyes. "This is wonderful, Mom, but what are we going to do with all this leftover cake?"

Amy slanted a glance his way as she took her first bite. "Funny that you should ask. We're expected at the Shared Blessings soup kitchen with cake in about an hour." She turned her head to include the Dentons in the conversation. "Everyone's invited to come help us serve. The staff there can use as many hands as they can get."

Dylan leaned over to Brad and Kelly again. "You never know what's going to happen when you get together with the Warrens and the Scotts."

Kelly gave him a warm smile as she covered her husband's hand with hers on the tabletop. "Yes, we do. Only good things."

Her words struck a place deep inside Dylan, making his throat feel thick. Strange, while they'd all been here celebrating together, he'd forgotten how they'd met Brad, Kelly and their sons in the first place. Somewhere along the way, they had become more than benefactors and beneficiaries. They had become friends.

"We wanted to thank all of you again," Kelly said. "You've done so much for us. You've helped to turn what could have been a very dark Christmas into a season of memories. You've given us hope."

Dylan didn't try to speak after that because there was no way he could do it without embarrassing himself by getting choked up. Jenna must have realized it, too, because she smiled at him from across the table. At one time, it would have bothered him to think she saw any sort of weakness in him, but he found that he didn't mind the transparency now.

"Don't you see?" Jenna glanced at Dylan as if to let him know she was speaking for all of them before she turned back to Kelly and Brad. "You're the ones who've given *us* hope. Meeting your family has been a blessing for us. You're amazing examples of faith. No matter how tough the situation has been, you've never wavered in your beliefs."

Finally finding his voice again, Dylan added. "You've helped to make this an amazing Christmas for us, so we want to thank *you*."

"The best Christmas ever," Logan agreed.

"Speaking of great holidays," Matthew said as he reached for Haley's hand, "my wife and I have some special Christmas news."

Before he had a chance to say more, Amy and Trina reached for each other, linking both their hands.

Haley grinned like someone who'd kept a secret too long. "As best as we can calculate, sometime in the late summer, a new little Warren will be arriving here."

"A baby!" The two mothers cheered together.

"A baby brother?" Lizzie's eyes were wide with excitement, and then she frowned. "Or a sister."

Laughter filled the room as everyone stood up to share congratulatory hugs with the expectant parents.

Dylan turned back to Brad and Kelly. "See what I mean? You never know what to expect."

Jenna, who'd just given her younger sister a squeeze, must have overheard him because she smiled at him from across the room, a look so warm he felt tremors all the way to his heels.

He never knew what to expect with this particular Scott woman, all right, from her transformation over the past few years to his heart's willingness to lay exposed for her benefit. Even if she frustrated him and terrified him and drew him to her despite his best efforts to resist her, he still loved the way she kept him guessing.

He swallowed and pulled his gaze away from her. He was in way over his head, and he knew it. Maybe he wasn't as ready for that promised talk with Jenna as he'd thought. But then the side of his mouth lifted. It didn't matter whether or not he was ready to confess his feelings. He could shout it from the rooftops or bury it deep inside him, but the truth would remain that Jenna Scott had again claimed his heart.

Chapter Fourteen

Jenna's muscles ached that Tuesday afternoon, even muscles she hadn't been aware existed until she'd stretched too high, stooped too low and hauled more boxes than anyone ever should. The delivery truck was gone now, but she needed only to look at the stack of boxes in any of the rooms for proof that their work had just begun.

Not that they hadn't already been working so hard since Christmas that the past few days had gone in a blur. She had the blisters and broken nails to prove it.

At the sound of the front door opening, Jenna stepped to the kitchen doorway, so she could see the entry. She patted her hair, trying to restore some order to her messy ponytail, but she didn't know why she made the effort. Dylan hadn't been working that much with her these past few days, anyway. He'd said he wanted to talk to her after Christmas, so it seemed odd that he hadn't yet. It made her wonder even more what he intended to say.

Dylan stuck his head inside the door. "Second shift reporting for duty."

Kelly hurried down the hall toward him. "Oh, good, because the rest of us have dinner reservations."

"Very funny," Brad said as he followed Dylan inside, but he bent and dropped a kiss on his wife's forehead. Unlike the rest of them, who were spending another day in their work clothes, Brad wore his Sunday best, though he'd already taken off his suit jacket and loosened his tie.

"Well, how did it go?" Jenna couldn't help asking.

"You mean the boys' eyeglass fitting?" Dylan lifted an eyebrow. "It went great."

They all knew that wasn't the question she'd asked, but they went with it as Dylan made a production of announcing the twins' entrance. They stepped inside, wearing their new wire-frame glasses, just different enough to show off their individuality.

"Oh, don't you two look handsome," their mother gushed as she hurried over to hug them. "So grown up."

The twins made those miserable faces that boys make when their mothers get too mushy. But her compliments must have given them courage, because they rushed off to show some of the others their new glasses.

After they left, Kelly turned back to Dylan. "Thanks again. It was so kind of you to persuade your bosses to cover the cost of their glasses."

"It wasn't a big deal. The boys needed them."

His gaze darted toward Jenna, but she looked away before he could see in her eyes that she knew. She found it precious that he hadn't shared that he'd covered the cost of the glasses himself, and she wanted him to be able to keep his secret.

Strange, how she'd found so many things endearing about him lately, just at the time when he'd started finding more excuses to put space between them. Not all the time. In fact, sometimes everything seemed okay between them, but then suddenly he would feel the need to work on plumbing with his brothers when he could have been painting doors in the garage with her.

Whether he was reluctant or not, they needed to talk about his gift and the conversation that had followed it, and even about the changes in their relationship.

Now aware that Dylan and Brad had returned, other helpers spilled from different parts of the house. Logan and Matthew had been installing the new electric range, and Jenna's sisters and the two older women had been unpacking boxes at the back of the house, but they all converged in the living room, hungry for information.

"Well, are you guys going to tell us about the interview or not?" Kelly crossed her arms over her chest.

Dylan tilted his head toward Brad. "What do you think? Should we tell them?"

At first, Brad nodded sadly, but then he grinned. "You're looking at the newest custodian at Sycamore Square Mall. After a probationary period, I can be considered for the custodial-supervisor position that's also open."

"Oh, thank you, Lord," Kelly called out as she threw her arms around her husband. "That's wonderful."

A round of hugs broke out as everyone celebrated Brad's new job. Jenna asked Dylan in a low voice, "Your shopping-center contacts?"

"Brad must have wowed them in the interview," he answered just as quietly.

She closed her arms around Dylan the way she'd hugged Brad a minute before and Dylan himself hundreds of times, but the wallop of sensations that filled her when his arms closed around her was something new. It was as if every nerve ending in her hands and arms, shoulders and back had activated at once, and she was left trying to catch her breath without appearing to suffer from an asthma attack.

The hug didn't seem long enough, but since Dylan had to extricate himself from her arms, it couldn't have been that short, either. He turned away quickly, but not quick enough for her to miss the surprise and confusion on his face.

Jenna could relate to that turmoil. If she were honest with herself, though, she would admit she had an idea about what was happening, and that idea scared her to death. Could she be falling in love with her best friend? She'd promised herself she wouldn't let it happen, and yet she couldn't deny that she was in deep now.

No, this feeling couldn't be love. Her impression that her heart expanded whenever Dylan entered a room and contracted when he left it again had to be an exaggeration. He was her friend, and she loved him. But still.

Clearly they needed to talk. At least then they could work out some of her confusion, delineate the boundaries of this new relationship, because for her at least, the lines had blurred.

Jenna looked at Dylan again, but the festive atmosphere from a few minutes before had disappeared. Brad was holding Kelly in his arms, rubbing her back while she sobbed against his chest.

"We're going to be okay," he crooned to her in a low voice. "Gonna be okay."

Jenna's breath caught. For more than a week while they'd all been working together, Kelly had been forced to be strong, but now that it appeared her family would be fine, she had released her hold on all those overwhelming emotions.

"Miss Jenna, why is Mommy crying?" Ryan asked her, tugging on her sleeve.

The worried faces of this sweet boy and his brother made her heart ache.

"You know, I think it's because she's happy."

He gave her a skeptical look and then turned to watch his parents again. Kelly must have heard the exchange because she pulled back from her husband's arms and started drying her tears. When she stepped over to her sons, her face was red and her eyes were puffy, but she was smiling.

"Miss Jenna's right, guys." She put her arms over the shoulders of both boys. "I *am* happy. Thanks to God and all these nice people, we have a house and clothes and food. All the things we need. Your dad even has a job so we can pay our own bills."

As she lowered her arms, she turned and crouched in front of her sons. "We're going to be all right. I wasn't so sure about that before."

"Why not, Mommy?" Connor wanted to know. "Didn't you have faith?"

"Sure, I—" She stopped herself and reached out to ruffle his hair. "I guess not."

For several seconds, no one spoke, and then Brad started chuckling. "Out of the mouths of babes, huh?"

As he grabbed both his sons and wrestled them under his arms, he turned to Matthew and Haley. "Everyone should have a few of these, don't you think?"

"Absolutely," Matthew answered.

Haley, who'd been green all day with morning sickness, only smiled.

"Yes, everyone should," Mrs. Warren agreed, though she was looking at Dylan and Caroline when she said it.

Caroline pretended to miss the comment, the way she usually did, and without looking at him to see him do it, Jenna knew Dylan would be rolling his eyes.

Soon the call of all those unpacked boxes sent them back to different parts of the house. Leaving kitchen organization to the older women and Kelly, Jenna worked in the boys' bedroom with Haley. Once Matthew and Dylan had mastered the directions for assembling the bunk-bed set, Jenna climbed to the top bunk and wrestled the linens and comforter into place.

She liked the idea that the Dentons would sleep in their beds tonight, instead of sleeping bags. Though Brad and Kelly had gratefully accepted their help with the move today and even with furniture assembly and unpacking tonight, they'd already politely suggested that they would take over the rest of the work.

Jenna was surprised by her bittersweet feelings over the end of the project, but it was time. Her family and the Warrens had done more than just accomplish their goal of making a nice Christmas for another family; they had helped them rebuild their lives.

Only ten days had passed, yet so much seemed to have changed, and not just for the family they had helped, either. Her mother and Mrs. Warren had brought their families together again this Christmas in hopes of them building stronger bonds. Jenna wondered if they realized how successful their plan had been.

No, the holidays hadn't turned out the way Mrs. Warren had envisioned them, but the results had to exceed her expectations. Not only had her children and her best friend's children connected in a way they never had before, but in sharing their holiday with a family in need, they had experienced the true spirit of Christmas.

"You go this way. I'll go that way." Dylan waited as Jenna took her position on the opposite side of the kitchen table.

"We'll get him this time," Jenna assured him.

"No you won't," Ryan ducked under the table and scrambled out the other side before either of them could catch him.

Connor ran into the room, already shirtless and barefoot. "He wins! He wins!"

"He's not going to be a winner for long if he doesn't get in the shower like your mom and dad said before they left."

Because there was a note of warning in Dylan's voice, Ryan glanced back to see if Dylan was serious. Dylan gave his best stern look to show that he was, though he hadn't a clue what he would tell the boys if they asked what his threat meant. It had sounded good at the time.

"What he means is, anyone who isn't clean, combed and in PJs in twenty minutes will have to skip popcorn and a video before bedtime," Jenna said.

The boys looked at each other for no more than a second and then both shot down the hall.

"I call the shower first!"

"I already have my clothes off!"

"Hey, boys, there are two showers," Dylan said. He looked back at Jenna. "Here, let me handle this."

"I'll just finish these." She indicated the few dishes in the sink from the macaroni-and-cheese and chicken-fingers dinner they'd just shared.

Resisting the urge to see anything warm and domestic in the scene, Dylan started down the hall after the racing ruffians. The boys weren't accustomed to living in a house with more than one bathroom, so they were used to the evening race. He had to smile at that thought. He and his brothers used to have a nightly bath race, too.

With a little negotiating, he had them both settled in separate bathrooms with pajamas, soap and shampoo. He was still smiling when he started down the hall to join Jenna again in the kitchen.

He didn't know why he'd let himself get all worked up about spending an evening alone with Jenna in the first place. They weren't even alone, unless they didn't count the 110 pounds of seven-year-olds who had kept them hopping from the time the boys' parents had backed out of the driveway. And if he was being technical, he would admit that he and Jenna had already been alone together in this house a few times in the past week.

But he had been nervous, so nervous that he'd had sweaty hands when he'd picked up Jenna at her mother's house. He hated feeling like a teenager on a first date when this didn't even qualify by the broadest sense of the word as a date.

His anxiety wasn't only about being with Jenna, or even being *alone* with Jenna. He was more worried about the conversation that would take place tonight, words that were long overdue. He'd been a coward this week, dodging Jenna to delay the talk. But he supposed his faintheartedness should only be expected since he'd made the suggestion in a rare moment of daring. He still wasn't sure he was ready to explain about his second gift or tell her how he felt, but he owed her something.

When he stepped into the kitchen, Jenna was still standing at the sink. She looked back at him. "You got both of them in the shower and you're still dry? I'm amazed."

"Well, you should be. What happened to those sweet little boys their parents left two hours ago?"

She lifted a handful of suds from the dishwater and blew them into the sink where she'd been rinsing. "Poof. They disappeared just like all well-behaved children do the moment the babysitter comes. I take it you didn't babysit much—oh, I guess I already knew that about you."

She smiled that smile that would still get to him even if he was catatonic. She did know him better than anyone else; that was something that had never changed.

"Here, let me help." He moved to the sink and grabbed a dish towel. "There's a dishwasher down there, you know." He pointed below the counter.

"But it's brand-new, and I don't want to be the first one to use it."

"Or to break it."

"That, too."

He was just drying the last dish when the twins rushed into the room, sporting pajamas and wet hair.

"Popcorn!" Ryan cheered.

"And movie!" Connor chimed in.

"And then bedtime," Dylan and Jenna said at the same time and laughed. That the kids didn't think it was funny only made them laugh harder.

By the time the last of the popcorn was gone and the movie credits had rolled, Dylan didn't know who was sleepier, the adults or the children, but the boys would never admit it. After piggyback rides to their room, some lengthy bedtime prayers and finally lights out, which involved leaving one closet light on, Dylan pulled their bedroom door closed, and he and Jenna trudged back to the kitchen.

"How do parents do it?" Jenna dropped into a kitchen chair and rested her head on her arms.

"I think they drag around just like this." He lowered himself into the chair opposite her.

"Well, I, for one, am amazed by them. Brad and Kelly in particular." She held her hands wide to indicate the room. "Can you believe they already have curtains up and pictures on the wall?"

"They do only have possessions collected in a week rather than over years, but it still was a lot of work putting them away."

"An incredible amount of work." She looked around again, and when she turned back to him, she was smiling. "They sure looked excited about going out tonight."

"It was a great Christmas present, wasn't it?"

"They could have warned us that the boys are like gremlins someone fed after midnight when they have a babysitter, but it still was good gift." She stifled a yawn. "I don't know about you, but I could veg out in front of the TV for the rest of the night."

Dylan glanced at her. Instead of looking back at him, she was studying her hands, folded together on the tabletop. She was giving him an out, and he knew it. He was tempted to take her up on it, too, to let the talking box keep them from really talking.

It was too easy, though, and he was sick of taking the easy way out.

"How about I make some tea, instead?" He took a deep breath and added, "Then we can talk."

Chapter Fifteen

Jenna wrapped her hands around the mug of hot tea that Dylan had placed in front of her and waited as he set out another for himself. Making tea had required some creativity, since the Dentons didn't have a kettle or a microwave yet—Dylan had boiled water in a saucepan and found two mismatched mugs on the cabinet's top shelf. He set a bowl of sugar and two spoons in the center of the table.

"Now that wasn't as easy as it sounded. I probably should have checked to see if there was any tea before I offered to make some."

Instead of taking the seat across the table so he would face her, he settled in the chair next to hers.

"I was worried that you'd have to go out and grow the tea leaves before you could brew a cup."

"Yeah, me, too."

Were they really sitting there talking about tea? What would be their next topic? Shelf liners? Jenna knew she should keep quiet and give him the chance to say whatever he'd planned to, but she couldn't help herself. She hated seeing him so uncomfortable as he appeared to search for the right words, especially when she had something she needed to say, as well.

She waited as long as she could, but she couldn't hold back anymore. "I'm sorry I stood you up on our first date."

Dylan blinked a few times, and then his tongue slipped out to moisten his lips. "Our first date?"

"I knew when you asked me that you were talking about a real date, not just hanging out." The sweet memory that popped into her head then made her smile. "You were so nervous…" She stopped, her gaze darting his way before she continued, "Anyway, I could tell that you'd worked up the courage to ask."

Jenna hated seeing the embarrassment on his face. She'd only just acknowledged the truth to herself, so it was harder to share it with him. "I wanted to go at first. It felt right. But then the misgivings started setting in, and I didn't know what to do."

"But why?"

She stirred her spoon around in her tea, though she hadn't put any sugar in it. "I chickened out. I knew that if we went out together and started a relationship, and then things didn't work out between us, I would lose my best friend. So when that other guy asked me out, the one who was the same kind of awful guy I always dated, it was an easy decision to cancel on you and go with him, instead."

He raised an eyebrow. "Easy?"

"The coward's way out."

Jenna braced herself, waiting for him to respond.

She deserved whatever he had to say and more for having treated his feelings so cavalierly to protect her own. She could have shielded herself by not telling him now, but he deserved to know the truth, no matter what it cost her.

Still, when he pushed back from the table, a fresh ache settled in her heart. She could only watch as he went into the laundry room and grabbed his coat off one of the wall hooks. Only he didn't put it on. He dug through the pockets, instead, his hand coming out with a white, letter-size envelope.

Hanging up his coat again, he returned to the table, set the envelope on top and slid it her way.

"What's this?" she asked as she rested her hand on it.

"Your other present. You know. The one I told you about." He swallowed. "You see why I picked the one with Christmas colors?"

She didn't see anything except the white envelope that he'd obviously been too nervous to give her. The birdhouse had been a substitute for whatever was inside that envelope.

"Aren't you going to open it?"

Jenna took a deep breath, not at all sure she was ready to see what was in there, but she pushed her thumb under the lip of the envelope and dragged it across.

She pulled out what appeared to be a letter written on lined paper, but when she unfolded it, she discovered it wasn't a letter at all. It was a poem, entitled simply "For Jenna." Yet it wasn't even recopied. The paper had yellowed, and all the words in the draft had just been marked out as he'd revised.

For Jenna
Roses are red, but not as red as her lips,
Violets are blue, never as blue as my heart.
When she calls me, my pulse trips,
To tell her, I don't know where to start.
I don't want to be just her friend.

Daisies are white like the white lies I've told,
Daffodils are yellow like the coward that's me.
She is the one I long to hold.
Will she never hear my heart's plea?
I don't want to be just her friend.

Her heart squeezed after she read those first two stanzas. Those were the musings of a lovesick adolescent, feeling hopeless and invisible. Jenna hated that she'd ever made him feel that way. She didn't want to read more, didn't want to know more of his pain and to realize she'd been the one responsible for it, but the words called out to her.

The room is aglow when she steps inside.
Her laughter heals old wounds like a salve.
From these feelings I can no longer hide.
An answer from her heart I must have.
I don't want to be just her friend.

Change has painted her lovelier throughout.
Her compassion seeks out those who are broken.
My heart waits for hers; I have no doubt.
These words I can no longer leave unspoken.
I don't want to be just her friend.
I want to be her man.

As soon as she read the last words, Jenna understood why he'd left the work as it was, instead of recopying it. This poem had been written at different times by two different people: the boy Dylan used to be and the man he'd become.

And suddenly she knew. She loved Dylan. She'd loved that sweet boy, and she loved the man even more. How could she not have known it before? How could she not have seen that what she'd always wanted had been right there in front of her eyes?

Dylan just might love her, too. At least that was what the poem seemed to say in black and white. He'd cared about her when they were teenagers, and he still did, no matter how much pain she'd caused him, no matter how unwise he believed his feelings to be.

For several long seconds Jenna could do nothing but stare at the weathered page, though her eyes began to fill. She brushed her hand over the smooth surface of the page, her fingertips following the dented places where he'd marked out the wrong words.

Dylan's gaze seemed to follow the slow slide of her hand. "I guess I'm not a great poet. Then or now."

"I think it's beautiful."

It took her a few seconds to gather the courage, but finally she looked up at him. His eyes were cautious, searching, as if he didn't know what he would find, but he had to know nonetheless.

"Thank you. I love it." Jenna didn't even stop to think. She leaned forward and pressed her lips to his.

It was the briefest of kisses, just a tentative touch, and yet it changed everything. Jenna pulled back and stared at him, her pulse ticking in her temple. Dylan looked as surprised as she felt, his eyes wide with unspoken questions. She could see the exact moment the surprise in his eyes turned to joy.

"I've waited my whole life for this," he whispered and then reached for her, his hands tracing from her forearms to her upper arms and then over her shoulders to settle at the back of her neck.

Dylan leaned in close and hovered, so close that she could feel his breath as a warm caress on her lips. This wasn't to be a kiss of gratitude, one to be explained away as a whim. In his hesitation, he was waiting for her consent, asking if this was something she really wanted. With a small smile, she granted her permission.

She didn't have to say it twice. He lowered his head and pressed his lips to hers in the sweetest, most loving kiss Jenna had ever experienced. A lifetime of adoration settled into that one moment, filled with hope and promise and love.

Dylan's heart raced as he held her, but he forced his kiss to remain unhurried. This was Jenna, the person who'd filled his thoughts and dreams for as long as he could remember. There was no rush. Kissing her felt like the answer to a lifetime of prayers, the one clear view in an otherwise foggy sky.

She tasted sweet, but then he'd always known she would, and he'd had a lot of years to predict. Not only smooth, her lips were also pillow soft, and he couldn't help but sink into their softness. He didn't even know when he deepened the kiss, only that he was expressing the feelings he'd held so long in his heart.

When he would have preferred to go on touching and

tasting, Dylan's good sense prevailed, and he pulled back, just far enough to press his forehead to hers.

"Do you have any idea how many times I've thought about this moment? How much I dreamed about holding you in my arms?" he breathed.

"Is the reality as nice as your dream?"

He couldn't help smiling, his mouth still just a breath away from hers. Even if he'd had a lot of basis for comparison, he knew that anything from his past would have paled when measured against this moment.

"Reality is perfect."

Her sweet smile then only made him long to kiss her again, so he took her hands in his and eased his forehead back from hers, putting a cushion of distance between them. The last thing he wanted to do was to lose firm control over his better judgment and cause her to believe he thought of her as anything less than precious.

"I tried to avoid you when you came back for the holidays, and I was so frustrated when you made it impossible." He sighed, shaking his head. "Even after I decided to forgive you, I still tried to keep you at arm's length. But no matter how many times I warned myself to be cautious, to separate friendship from any closer relationship, I ignored the warnings.

"As absurd as it sounds, something inside me kept asking, if you and I were both different now, then why *not* now?"

For several seconds Jenna said nothing, looking at him with a wide-eyed expression. He'd gone too far, and he knew it. Why couldn't he just have seen the gift in her kiss and accepted that it would be a journey of baby steps toward a dating relationship between them?

Now he'd pushed her, and she would probably go running in the opposite direction.

"Not absurd."

"What did you say? I didn't understand you." He thought he'd heard her, but she'd said it so quietly that he couldn't have heard her right.

"I said it's not absurd."

He would have demanded that she explain what she meant by that, but he couldn't trust himself to speak. Like the words of a jury foreman, the next thing that Jenna said would either be a gift for the future or a sentence to a life without her.

The look on her face as she met his gaze made him brace himself for news that would hurt. Her eyes shone too brightly, as if she was only a comment away from tears. But then she smiled, and the clouds in his heart separated, allowing the sun to shine through.

"You're right. Why *not* now?"

"I can't believe we were almost busted." Jenna shook her head and smiled as Dylan pulled the car to the curb in front of her mother's house.

She still felt a little jittery after tonight's events, but she pushed aside her uncertainties. He was still Dylan, and she was still Jenna. Only their relationship was in flux.

"Just like a couple of teenage babysitters." He shut off the ignition and turned in the driver's seat to face her. "Not that Brad and Kelly would have found anything all that shocking if they had busted us. Just a kiss."

"They wouldn't have been that surprised, either."

"What do you mean?"

"Kelly's always wondered about us. Ever since that first day at breakfast."

Dylan drummed his fingers against the steering wheel. "After that scene tonight, she's probably more curious."

"Why would you say that?"

"We had to look suspicious when we both jumped up from the table after Brad and Kelly came through the door."

Jenna frowned. "What do you mean? We were just picking up because they were home and we needed to get going."

"You told them the boys were sleeping like 'little baby lambs.'"

"Do you think it was overkill?" She thought about it for a second. "Don't worry. They probably thought I was kidding, anyway."

"Either way. But this does bring up another subject. What are we going to tell everyone else?"

"You mean about—" she paused, gesturing back and forth between them "—us?"

"Yeah."

She shot a look at her mother's front door, illuminated by a pair porch lights and the glow of the living-room lamp her mother would have left on for her. The house appeared quiet, so she turned to Dylan again. "We haven't even defined what 'us' is yet. Or even if there is an 'us.'" She shook her head. "And I have to fly back to Detroit in a few days."

"Maybe it would be best if we wait a while to share, at least until we figure out what to say." Though Dylan suggested it, he didn't sound as if the idea would have been his first choice.

"That's probably a good idea. Just a few days…to see." To see what exactly, she wasn't sure. If they could survive as a couple that long? A few days were hardly the test of a relationship's endurance.

"Our moms will probably be disappointed, anyway." He lifted a shoulder and let it fall. "You aren't Caroline, and she was part of their plan."

In a huff, she turned in her seat to face him, crossing her arms over her chest. "And why Caroline in the first place? I'm not saying she's not amazing. She is. But how could our mothers ever have thought she was right for you?"

"You know how they are," he said with a shrug. "If they had the ability to look at the big picture, they wouldn't be trying to set up their kids at all."

"I just hate that they've made you the consolation prize for Caroline because Matthew and Haley ended up together. I mean, not that Caroline ever wanted a consolation prize. She doesn't want any guy." After the first vehement comment and all of that backtracking, Jenna glanced at him sheepishly, glad he couldn't see her blush in the darkness of the car.

It was to his credit that he didn't laugh. When he finally spoke, he didn't make a single wisecrack.

"You've defended me ever since you arrived here, and our mothers' new game began. I really appreciate that. You really have been a good friend to me. Thank you for that."

Jenna blinked. There were so many things he could have said to her, but this one touched her more than anything else could have. She'd returned to see him here, hoping to restore the friendship of their past, and she'd surpassed that goal, becoming the kind of friend he deserved.

He must have understood how his words moved her because he continued without waiting for a response. "You know, it was unfair of our mothers to change their game plan just because my big brother ended up married to your baby sister. Remember in their master plan, they talked about the two oldest, two youngest and two—"

"Middle," they said at the same time and laughed.

As their laughter died, Jenna sensed that the atmosphere in the car had changed, had become more intimate. For what felt like a long time, neither spoke, but she could sense his gaze on her, and she couldn't help peeking back at him.

Finally Dylan shifted in his seat. "We'd better get you inside." Instead of waiting for her answer, he opened his car door and then hurried around to the passenger side to open the door for her.

Jenna swallowed, feeling more nervous than she had even for her senior prom. But when Dylan held out his hand to her, she didn't hesitate to take it. Laced through hers, his fingers felt warm, even through her thin gloves. The temperature outside had dropped another ten degrees with promise of a white New Year's, but Jenna didn't even feel the cold. This was Dylan, the friend of her childhood and the surprise of her adult life. She felt warm just being next to him.

On the porch Dylan turned her to face him. She was tempted to glance at the front window to catch her mother watching as she always had whenever Jenna had gone on a date. But this wasn't a date, only a baby-sitting job. Her mother wouldn't have any reason to snoop. She wouldn't even be worried about Jenna when stable Dylan was there to make sure she made it home safely.

"Are you okay? Warm enough?"

Dylan stroked her cheek with the back of his fingers as he asked, and Jenna could have assured him that she wasn't the slightest bit cold. She looked up into those warm, chocolate eyes, and she nodded. This was the man she'd always known. The one she'd always loved, but she'd been too afraid to admit it.

Stepping closer to her and shielding her from the wind with his body, he settled his hands on her coat at her waist and bent until their faces were only inches apart.

"I really want to kiss you again, Jenna. Would you like me to do that?"

Jenna had been staring into his amazing eyes, but at his words, she blinked. He hadn't asked for permission. Instead, he wanted to know what she wanted. It was so like him to worry about her feelings, even when it would have been so easy for him to overcome any reluctance and muddle her brain with his kiss. He wanted her to come to him of her own free will.

His kindness in itself would have been enough to win her over, even if she wasn't already willingly tumbling headfirst into his eyes. "I'd like that." She expected her voice to come out shaky, but it sounded strong.

By small increments, Dylan moved closer until a tilted chin would be enough to bring their lips together. Jenna closed that distance herself. As their lips touched,

Dylan's arms closed around her in an embrace that shut out the world. Rather than just a touch of lips, Dylan's gentle kiss felt like the promise of a lifetime together. She wanted nothing more than to be able to accept his offer.

Too soon he lifted his head away and took a step back from her, his hands still resting on her waist.

"Well, good night." He glanced at something over her shoulder. "Did you see that?"

"See what?"

"The curtain moved."

Jenna swallowed. "Oh." She looked from the window to the door and back to the window. What was she supposed to do now? The idea of being with Dylan was new. She wasn't ready to share it with the others, but now she wouldn't have a choice.

"Let's go." Dylan held out a hand to her. He pulled open the door so quickly that he caught Jenna's mother and Mrs. Warren before they could jump back from the window.

Amy jerked her hand to her chest. "Dylan, you just startled the life out of me."

"Me, too," Trina agreed.

"Could be that you were too close to the window," Dylan answered in a flat tone.

"Perhaps." Amy smiled at her best friend. "But it was worth the shock."

Instead of saying more, their matchmaking moms just stared at their offsprings's joined hands with self-satisfied grins, as if they'd arranged the whole budding romance between them.

"You knew all along?" Jenna couldn't help asking.

Trina grinned at her daughter. "Well, not all along, but—"

"But nothing," Dylan said with a chuckle. "You didn't have any idea."

His mother smiled at her son first and then at Jenna before lowering her gaze again to their joined hands. "But we did plant the garden. Only God gets to decide which things grow."

Chapter Sixteen

For the tenth time in the past fifteen minutes, Dylan took his gaze off the checkers game he was supposed to be playing with Logan and looked out the living-room window, searching for car lights. The snow had start fluttering down early in the afternoon, and now, just in time for New Year's Eve traffic, it was coming down in earnest. Jenna, Caroline and their mother should have already arrived, and the wait was killing him.

With another look up the street, he turned back to his brother and the game. Logan grinned at him as he executed a triple jump that landed his game piece on the opposite side of the board.

"King me." Sitting on the floor next to the coffee table where they'd arranged the game, Logan leaned back on his elbows as Dylan turned away again. "Either pay attention or this is going to be a really short game."

"What?" Dylan looked back from the window. "Oh. Sorry."

"Relax, man. She'll be here." He coughed into his hand. "I mean they'll all be here. It's the Warren family New Year's Eve movie marathon. Who would miss that?"

"Yeah, who would?"

Dylan didn't even bother wondering how his younger brother knew about the *she* who would be there. No one in either of their families could keep a secret. This time he didn't even want it to be a secret. After all these years of first hiding how he felt and then pretending he didn't feel it, he couldn't wait for tonight, when they would attend the party as a couple. He didn't have to hide anything anymore.

But more than having the chance to announce that he'd begun a relationship with the woman of his dreams, he couldn't wait to see her. He looked forward to the stroke of midnight, too, when he could gather her in his arms again.

"Dylan, I'm killing you here." Logan pointed to the game, where another of his pieces was prepared to be kinged. "Jenna's really muddled your brain again, hasn't she?"

"Just like in high school," Matthew added.

Dylan was just registering that Matthew had returned from the kitchen, where he'd been helping their mother and Haley with the appetizers, when he realized what his brothers had said. Both of them. He stood up from the sofa, which he'd been using as his perch to watch for arriving guests.

"Aw, come on, buddy," Logan said. "We're your brothers. Did you really think we didn't notice how you used to moon over Jenna? Or how you'd hide in your room for days every time she smashed your heart like a bug by telling you about another new boyfriend?"

Matthew shook his head, chuckling. "Nobody could be as good a friend as you were to her through all those breakups if he didn't secretly hope she'd wake up and smell the coffee and finally see him there waiting for her."

Dylan looked back and forth between his brothers, humiliation welling in his veins. He'd thought he'd done such a good job of hiding how he felt, and now he learned he'd been a miserable failure.

Logan must have recognized they'd stepped on sensitive ground with their comments because he held his hands wide. "But hey, look who won out in the end. Mom said you two looked pretty close on the porch last night."

Dylan could feel the heat creeping up his neck. "If you two knew all that stuff before, why didn't you ever say anything about it to me?"

"A guy has the right to a little privacy with his misery," Logan told him.

"What can we say? We're guys." Matthew strode over to Dylan and gave his back two firm pats. "And we were already in the habit of hiding our feelings about Dad. We were good at avoiding communication by that time."

"Too bad you couldn't stick with that now," Dylan joked, and they all laughed.

But he wasn't really kidding. His brothers' comments had struck too deep. He needed no reminders that he'd always cared for Jenna more than she had for him, that he'd always been the one more invested in their relationship.

He hated that one conversation could cause his misgivings to reappear, but that was all it took. Would he always be the one with more to lose if he allowed his relationship with Jenna to move forward? He didn't want to answer yes to that question, but he couldn't say a positive no, either.

A relationship should be based on trust, and yet he wasn't certain he could ever trust her completely. Would he allow his heart to be that bug Logan so eloquently described, the one just waiting to be smashed again?

"They're here," Lizzie called out as she came running into the room.

Sure enough, like the proverbial watched pot that never boils, Mrs. Scott's car had pulled into the driveway at the very moment he wasn't staring out the window and waiting. Unfortunately that also meant that the woman he loved had also just arrived, right when he wasn't ready to see her.

Beside him, his niece was chattering on about how Grammy had told her she could pick out the first movie, but Dylan was focused on that car and the woman climbing out of it.

Even with just her eyes, nose and cheeks peeking out from the fluffy faux fur of her hood, Jenna still looked so pretty that Dylan couldn't take his eyes off her as she hurried up the walk. Her mother and sister trailed behind her, taking more care to walk without slipping on the ice.

He had already started toward the front door when Lizzie pulled at his hand. "Uncle Dylan, is Aunt Jenna your girlfriend?"

Matthew nabbed his daughter under his arm so that

her arms and legs were dangling. "Hey, let's check out what kind of cakes Grammy has for the party." He headed toward the kitchen without giving his child a chance to get an answer.

Dylan reached the door before Jenna could ring the bell. He pushed open the storm door and stepped back for her to come inside.

"Hey there."

"Hi." She paused awkwardly as if she thought he might greet her with a hug or a kiss, but then she stepped past him, slipped off her shoes and removed her coat.

Caroline and Mrs. Scott followed her inside, and though both looked back and forth between Dylan and her with curious expressions, neither commented on what they saw. Caroline smiled his way, probably a sign of gratitude for finally letting her off the hook in their mother's matchmaking game. Then the two of them continued into the kitchen.

He glanced around, surprised to see that the others had made themselves scarce, as well, probably hiding in the dining room or kitchen. Touching the back of Jenna's arm because he couldn't bear not to touch her for long, he guided her into the formal living room.

She turned a full circle. "Do you get the feeling no one wants to be around us?"

"They must be trying to give us some space."

Her beautiful mouth curved. "That's kind of them."

"Yeah, it is." But he couldn't look at her when he said it.

"Is something wrong?"

"Everything's fine," he said automatically.

When he glanced back at her, she was staring at her

stockinged feet. He never remembered her being shy or bashful, but she seemed that way now. Vulnerable. Despite his uncertainties, he hated that he would ever make her doubt how he felt. He would have had to be pinned to the wall to keep from drawing her into his arms and pressing a kiss to her hair.

Jenna released the breath she'd been holding as his arms closed around her. For a moment she'd been worried that something might have changed since she'd talked to Dylan on the phone earlier in the day, but with his arms around her now, her world righted itself. She'd thought he was looking forward to their chance to spend New Year's Eve together as much she'd been, but the truth was, she didn't know what he was feeling.

Maybe he was just uncomfortable sharing these early moments of their new relationship with all their relatives. She couldn't blame him for that. She had to expect some awkwardness in their transition, but strangely, she didn't feel embarrassed at having the others see them together. With Dylan she had finally seen the truth that had always been in her heart, and she no longer had any desire or will to hide from it.

A few days ago she wouldn't have allowed herself to think about a possible future with Dylan, and now she couldn't think about anything else. Just as her life didn't make sense without him in it, a romantic future for the two of them together made more sense than anything ever had.

Jenna would like to have discussed that future with him, but the others returned then, putting an end to their private moment. It was just as well. She would probably have rushed Dylan just when he needed them both to relax and take a breath.

"Aunt Jenna, Uncle Dylan didn't tell me. Is he your boyfriend?" Lizzie asked as soon as she reached them.

Jenna glanced sidelong at Dylan and then down at the preschooler. "We're really good friends. I know that."

Matthew scooted over and wrapped his arm around his daughter's shoulders. "Now, kiddo, what did I say earlier about asking people such personal questions?"

Instead of making everyone more uncomfortable, the child's question seemed to put them all at ease. Jenna knew she'd answered right, because no matter what else they were or what they might become together, she and Dylan were friends, and over the past two weeks, they'd become better ones.

They gathered in the family room for movie night, complete with snacks and, of course, one of Mrs. Warren's cakes, this time devil's food. Because Jenna dreaded the moment their mothers would begin the third degree about her budding relationship with Dylan, Jenna appreciated that the movie format for the New Year's Eve party didn't offer many opportunities for chatter.

They all took their seats on the sectional, and as she'd hoped, Jenna ended up seated next to Dylan. Through the first movie, a short, animated flick Lizzie picked to watch before bedtime, Jenna was too distracted to even watch the colorful characters.

She couldn't focus when Dylan was so close she could smell his woodsy cologne and brush his shoulder if he shifted in his seat. His hand was mere inches from hers, but he never reached out to take hers the way she hoped he would. She tried to tell herself he was simply trying not to be too public with displays of affection, but the thought didn't ring true, since he'd held her hand in front of their mothers last night.

When she caught sight of exhausted mom-to-be Haley resting her head on Matthew's chest, Jenna reminded herself she would only have to wait for the strike of midnight for Dylan and her to have a special moment of their own.

"Okay, everyone, it's almost time," Mrs. Warren announced as she distributed New Year's party hats and noisemakers.

"Ten…nine…eight…seven…six…"

Jenna counted down with the others, but her gaze was on Dylan. He caught her watching him, and his lips curved, but his smile didn't reach his eyes.

"Five…four…three…two…one. Happy New Year!" they all shouted.

Everyone jumped up and started exchanging hugs. When Dylan stepped her way, Jenna turned to face him, waiting for the kiss they would share in front of the others, the one that would make a statement about a possible future between them.

"Happy New Year, Jenna."

"Happy New Year." Her eyes fluttered closed in anticipation, but all he gave her was a brief kiss on the cheek. She glanced away so he wouldn't see the disappointment in her eyes, only to catch newlyweds Matthew and Haley sharing a sweet kiss.

Releasing her shoulders, he stepped away from her and gave Caroline the same kiss on the cheek he'd given Jenna. He did the same thing three more times with Haley and then his mother and hers.

Jenna tried not to let his actions bother her as she shared hugs with the others. He hadn't ignored her, just treated her exactly like everyone else whcn she'd wanted to be special. She was probably overreacting, anyway, just being paranoid because she'd taken a risk by getting involved with him.

His mixed messages confused her, though. Last night he'd given her every reason to believe he loved her. The poem was proof enough. But tonight he seemed to be pushing her away with both hands. What had happened between then and now?

With the midnight celebration complete, Amy prepared to start the next movie. There would be at least one more feature before their party broke up so they could all crawl into their beds. But before Dylan could sit again, Jenna touched his arm. "Could we talk for a minute?" She indicated the doorway to the hall with a nod of her head.

Dylan glanced around the room, but finally he nodded.

Jenna led him into the living room and turned to face him. "I don't understand. Something's wrong, isn't it? Tell me what it is."

He shook his head and started to deny it, but then he stopped. "Do you want to go for a drive with me?"

She shot a look at the front window where the snow continued to fall and was beginning to blow. "In that?"

"I have an SUV, remember?"

Within a few minutes, they had informed the others, endured all the speculative glances, grabbed their coats and headed out into the snow. She waited, but he didn't take her hand this time, either, even when no one else could see.

It didn't do any good for her to tell herself she was overreacting this time. She couldn't convince herself that she was imagining things or that everything was okay between them. As the snow crunched beneath the car tires, her heart filled with dread.

Dylan stopped the SUV in the parking lot of the supermarket three blocks from his mother's house. Though inside the store was dark, parking-lot lamps still poured their full light over the nearly empty lot, illuminating the interior of the SUV.

The location mirrored the conversation that was about to take place, Dylan decided, because in both he felt completely exposed.

"I thought this place never closed," Jenna said as she looked to the store window.

"It doesn't except on Easter, Christmas and New Year's Eve." He didn't know why they were having this inane conversation when there were more important things they needed to say.

She stared out the windshield into the emptiness of the parking lot. Her arms were wrapped tightly about herself as if to provide protection from an onslaught. He wanted to take her in his arms and protect her from anyone who would hurt her, and it shocked him to realize he would be battling himself. But her hurt would only be temporary, he reminded himself, just a scratch compared to the pain he could foresee in his own heart.

Finally Jenna unfastened her seat belt and turned

in her seat to face him. "Okay. Are you going to tell me now?"

"I don't know what it is," he began, but he realized that wasn't quite true. He did know. He just wasn't sure how to share it.

"Well, it's something." She still had her arms crossed but more in frustration now than for protection. "Last night you told me…well, you know what you told me. And the gift you gave me…" She turned away and cleared her throat before she tried again. "And then tonight after you knew full well that everyone there knew about us, you didn't want to be anywhere near me. It doesn't make sense. What changed?"

"Why was I never enough for you before?"

Dylan wasn't even sure he'd spoken the words aloud until he saw the confusion on her face. Confusion, then shock, then guilt. He'd never expected to pose that critical question to her aloud, and he felt trapped by it. He didn't want to know her answer, but then he couldn't bear not knowing, either.

Maybe his earlier conversation with his brothers had triggered some of his misgivings today, but if he was honest with himself, he would admit he'd always had questions. The one he'd asked Jenna tonight had never been far from his mind. Now that their relationship had changed, he needed that answer more than ever.

Jenna swallowed, her eyes and nose burning. She tried to meet his gaze, but he only stared out the driver's-side window. Guilt flooding her veins, she stared at her gripped hands.

"Why would you ever think you weren't enough?" Before he could answer, though, she shook her head to tell him she wouldn't need an answer. She'd probably given him dozens of reasons over the years, the primary being the date that never happened.

Only now did she begin to realize how much she'd hurt Dylan again and again. How could she have been so blind? She'd been so careless with his heart that he'd begun to question his own worth. This amazing, brilliant man had started second-guessing himself because of her. Worse than just knowing she'd hurt him was the reality that she couldn't take any of it back.

"I'm so sorry, Dylan."

"I thought it wouldn't matter," he seemed to say as much to himself as to her. "But when Matthew and Logan started kidding me about my pining after you when we were kids, I started remembering that. And then I remembered other things I would have preferred to forget."

Now she understood what had changed in a day's time. Maybe he'd believed, as she had, that their history wouldn't touch them now, but they'd both been wrong. She didn't want him to relive the pain she'd caused him then, but Dylan deserved an answer to his question, so she braced her hand on the armrest and began.

"It amazes me sometimes how selfish I was back then." He didn't look at her, but from the way his hands flexed and unflexed on the steering wheel, she could tell he was listening.

"Part of me always knew how you felt about me. I hate admitting that, but it's true. I didn't acknowledge your feelings because I was afraid if I did, I would lose you."

"Why were you afraid of that?" He still didn't look at her as he asked it.

She took a deep breath and pressed on to the hardest part of what she had to say. "As long as I didn't recognize your feelings, I wouldn't have to admit that I didn't feel the same way about you. I could still have you and all the boys I dated. I didn't want to give up...either."

By the last word, her voice faltered. How could she have been such a terrible person? She didn't know why he'd ever decided to be her friend again, let alone consider building a more tender relationship with her.

Dylan cleared his throat, his fingers never releasing the steering wheel "I appreciate your telling me." His voice sounded flat, resigned, as though if he hadn't made any permanent decision before, he'd made one now.

"But, Dylan, I'm not that person anymore. You know that. We're both different now. We'll be different together."

"But is *now* really that different?"

She'd been staring at her hands, but his strange question brought her head up again. "What do you mean?"

"You knew what you didn't want then. How would I ever know whether I was what you really wanted? I might have once been willing to settle for the crumbs in your life, but I'm not that guy anymore. I won't be the man you settle for."

"You've got to know that I'm not settling. I want you. I *choose* you."

"How could I ever know that for sure?"

Jenna opened her mouth to tell him he had to trust her, but the sad reality caused her to close it again as anguish twisted in her heart. Of course he couldn't count on her feelings for him. There was no way he would know for sure that she had chosen him, instead of ended up with him by default. How could they build any sort of a relationship when he would always wonder if her feelings were real or fleeting?

"I don't want to be anybody's safety net," Dylan continued when she didn't answer his question. "Do you understand that? Not even yours."

"But you're not a safety net. I—I really care about you. You have to know that." She'd almost told him she loved him, but she'd never said that aloud and she wasn't ready. Would he even believe her if she told him that now?

"You've always cared about me the way that best friends care about each other. But you also wanted to be around me because I was safe. You might even think there's more to us now because you lost that friendship for a while and found it again." He shook his head slowly.

"Don't you see? I can't do it. I don't want to be anyone's consolation prize. I want to be someone's everything."

Settling her elbows on her knees, Jenna held her head in her hands. "No, Dylan. It's not like that." But even she couldn't say that for sure. Her feelings for him—or at least her recognition of those feelings—were still too new for her to have analyzed them.

But she did want to be with him, so much it hurt.

Jenna didn't know when she started crying, but suddenly her cheeks were wet. As she lowered hands and leaned back against the headrest, Dylan reached over and wiped away a few of those tears.

"I'm sorry, Jenna. I don't mean to hurt you, but I

can't do this relationship thing. And for a while at least, I can't be your friend, either."

Jenna sniffled and then nodded. *I don't want to be just her friend.* The line from his poem filtered into her thoughts again, but those words did no more to change their situation than anything else she'd said tonight had. As Dylan drove her back to her mother's house, offering her the chance to skip the end of the holiday party, she reflected on how close she'd come to having everything she'd ever wanted.

It wouldn't be a happy new year, after all.

Chapter Seventeen

Jenna woke with a start in the late morning of New Year's Day, surprised she'd slept at all. Her eyes gritty from crying, she stared at the floral wallpaper in the guest room of her mother's house, which would never be home to her.

It had only been a few hours since Dylan had backed out of her mother's driveway, but already she missed him so much that all her muscles ached with loss. He was the one man who'd ever really mattered in her life.

If only she'd have realized her true feelings for Dylan sooner. Maybe then she wouldn't have caused so much damage, so much hurt, that she couldn't take it back no matter how much she'd changed.

Vaguely she took note of the light spilling in from the open drapes, not from sunlight but from the glare off the snow. Movement next to the window caught her attention. Blinking, she sat up in bed. Still dressed in her flannel pajamas and a robe, Caroline sat in the oak rocker.

"What are you doing in here?"

"Mom wanted me to check on you," Caroline said with a knowing smile. It wasn't uncommon for their mother to send one of the sisters in as a surrogate when situations promised to be too emotional for her comfort zone. "She thought this situation might be messy, but I assured her that you'll survive."

Jenna pushed a hand back through her hair, which felt like it was going every which way. "I'm fine."

"You don't look fine."

"Thanks. I feel better already."

"Glad to be of service. So what happened? I thought Mom's current matchmaking target for me was suddenly off the market, much to my chagrin, of course, and then he showed up back at his mother's house alone and refusing to talk to anyone."

"Sorry I messed up your reprieve." Jenna tried to smile but didn't quite manage it. "I assure you Dylan's still available."

"Are you kidding? Even if I was interested, which I'm not, that poor man is definitely *not* available." Caroline frowned as she tucked her feet under her in the chair. "Dylan's never been available. Why I never noticed it before, I'm not sure. I'm usually more observant than that."

"It doesn't matter, anyway, now. The relationship that took fifteen years to kindle took about fifteen hours for me to destroy."

"You?" Her sister popped out of the chair and climbed onto the bed to sit facing Jenna and holding her hands. "Dylan was the one giving you the cold shoulder last night when you were shining like a new penny."

Jenna shook her head, refusing to accept her sister's loyal defense. "No, it was my fault. I'd done so much damage years ago that I didn't need to do anything new to cause everything to collapse." She tried to pull her hands away, but her sister wouldn't let go.

"Do things you did a long time ago really matter that much now?"

"Dylan said I always wanted to be around him because he was safe, and I think he was right. Not only was he the polar opposite of any of the guys I ever dated, but he had these bookish, nerdy qualities that made him a little embarrassing." She closed her eyes, smiling at the memory of that awkward boy.

"I remember. He and Matthew were both kind of nerdy."

When Jenna opened her eyes, her sister was smiling back at her.

"All those things made him off-limits for me as a boyfriend. Safe, like he said," Jenna continued. "I could always love him without worrying he would leave me. But then he did leave me after he finally asked me out and I stood him up."

"You mean about four years ago?" Caroline had an incredulous expression on her face. "Well, then. Better call the rest of us chronically unobservant."

"What are you talking about?"

"How could we have missed that Dylan was in love with you? How could Mom and Mrs. Warren, who've been doing all this crazy matchmaking, have missed that they had a match in the bag?"

Jenna pulled her hands away. "Only it won't work.

Last night Dylan asked me why he was never enough before. He's decided he can't be with me because he doesn't want to be the guy I settled for. He's wrong— I know what I want now, but I'm too late. He'll never be able to know for certain that he's the one I really want." She hated that the tears started again, but she couldn't stop them.

Caroline reached out and brushed away a few of them. "Trust. That's a tough one."

"Without it, any relationship is impossible," Jenna said as she wiped at the tears that kept coming.

"Impossible, huh?" When Jenna lifted an eyebrow, Caroline continued, "I know you say you've found faith, but is it really true?"

"Of course it is."

"Then you might want to think about what Jesus said in Mark 10:27. 'With men it is impossible, but not with God; for all things are possible with God.'"

Jenna opened her mouth to retort, but then her lips curved into a smile. "Thanks. I'll keep that in mind."

"It probably seems unwise to be taking relationship advice from someone who isn't in a relationship and has no intention of being in one, but I do know a little about getting what you want out of life."

"And I appreciate your advice. Really." Jenna leaned forward and hugged her sister.

"You said you know what you want. Now you have to decide what you're going to do about it," Carline said.

She was right, Jenna decided as her sister left the room, probably to report to their mother that all was well. Jenna didn't want to give up now that she realized she and Dylan belonged together. She had to believe that it might be possible someday for her to earn his trust. But even if she didn't, he would always hold the key to her heart.

Dylan felt so alone as he sat at the kitchen table in his apartment, eating soup and staring out at the dark sky. His life had never felt more bleak or lonely. The first day of the new year had passed in a long series of gray minutes.

Part of him felt his decision to cut his losses with Jenna before there were any more of them was justified, unavoidable even, but the other part worried he'd made a huge mistake.

Jenna, the one woman he'd ever loved, was finally ready to be with him, and all he could do was turn her away with excuses about safety nets and consolation prizes. Why had he let his misgivings get to him in the first place? His brothers might have been encouraging him to proceed with caution, but he was certain they hadn't been going for this outcome.

He knew he shouldn't feel guilty for walking away from a woman who hadn't even been able to say that she loved him, but that offered him no comfort. Jenna had only recently recognized her feelings. He'd known how he felt for years, and he'd never said the words aloud, either.

The hopelessness he'd seen on her face when he'd told her they couldn't be together had almost been his undoing. He'd longed to hold her and tell her he was wrong, but the idea that she would change her mind someday over another rugby player or, more likely now, a pilot on one of her flights, had helped him keep his hands on the steering wheel.

He knew he'd hurt her. Were they even now? Was that what he needed, for them to be even? Would he feel comforted in his justice next Easter, next Fourth of July and next Christmas when he was still missing her?

His challenge, though, remained just where it had been before. How could he be sure that she wouldn't change her mind? Faith. The word came to him in a small voice from inside. Jenna had found faith, and then she'd helped him to open his heart to his own again. Maybe God could help him to have a little faith in her.

Lord, please give me the strength to follow my heart, if it's where You're leading. And teach me to have faith in the people I love, too. In Your Son's name I pray. Amen.

He had another long night of sleeplessness ahead of him, but he needed the time for prayer and for intro-spection. He needed time to find the courage to do what he knew was right.

Jenna sat in the terminal at Indianapolis International, early for her late-night flight. She was almost relieved to be surrounded by throngs of post-holiday travelers, all equally exhausted and crabby. At least when she was being elbowed and stepped on and tripped while walking barefoot through airline security, she wouldn't think of Dylan and the fact that he hadn't called all day.

Not that she knew what she would say if he did call. That he'd made a mistake was too much to ask. But she hadn't heard a word from him or from any of the other Warrens, including her own sister, Haley. At least Haley had an excuse—Jenna had heard she was suffering from worse morning sickness and had spent the day in bed.

Though Jenna wasn't looking forward to returning to her lonely apartment, she would appreciate the chance to be out of her mother's and Caroline's curious study. They were only concerned, but she felt like a bug under glass, waiting for the oxygen to run out.

At least now she could stop coming up with new versions of her harebrained plan to go to his house and convince him they could find a way to be together. She'd picked up her keys and dialed half of Dylan's number so many times today that her fingers ached almost as much as her heart. Her plans were courageous, but her execution was not.

The advantage of being at the airport early also turned out to be a disadvantage in that she had even more time to think, more time to ruminate on the reality that he hadn't called. If there was any hope for them, he would have by now.

Sitting in the uncomfortable chair, she held her head in her hands as her hope dwindled in small increments. What would she do now? She'd come to Markston hoping to reconnect with her friend, and she was leaving more alone than ever. She reminded herself that she'd lost more love in a matter of days than some people do in a lifetime, but somehow it didn't make her feel any better.

As she reached her lowest point, she pulled the smaller of her two Christmas gifts from Dylan out of her purse. She'd tried to fit the birdhouse in, too, but eventually gave up and gave her mother money to ship it. Just holding the folded-up paper made her feel better somehow. Even if Dylan no longer felt these tender feelings for her, there was a time he had.

She opened the poem and began to read what she'd read so many times in the last twelve hours.

Roses are red, but not as red as her lips,
Violets are blue, never as blue as my heart…

Sure, some of those thoughts had been written by a lovesick teen, but the others, the ones that mattered more, Dylan had written only recently.

I don't want to be just her friend.
I want to be her man.

By the time she reached the final line, her hope had returned. His words reminded her that he'd loved her. If he still did, there had to be a chance for them. Jumping up from her seat, she rushed over to the flight desk to request that her bag be removed from the luggage bin.

Blood pumped at her temples. She couldn't walk fast enough out of the secured part of the terminal to the car-rental department.

For once, though, her plan was more about Dylan's needs than hers. No matter what Dylan felt about her now, whether he was willing to accept her or not, there were things she had to tell him in the morning. Things that meant the world to her and, if God willed it, could mean a future for the two of them.

As Dylan merged onto Interstate 465 the next morning, anticipation and anxiety melded inside him, making it difficult to watch for the signs to Indianapolis International. There was more traffic than usual on the last Saturday before the end of the traditional Christmas vacation, but he was still sure he would make his flight on time. He'd been blessed to get a last-minute ticket, but since he was heading north, instead of the warmer south, he'd found a seat.

The plan was crazy, but taking the risk felt exhilarating. He wasn't even sure where she lived, but he would figure all that out when he landed in Detroit.

He could almost picture the surprise on her face when he showed up at her apartment. He had so much to tell her, things he'd never said, things he should have said if he hadn't been such a coward.

In all the years he'd loved Jenna, he'd never once made it clear what he wanted. Today he would make it clear. He'd never told her he loved her for fear she would reject him. Today he would tell her. He would no longer allow fear and pride to keep him from taking a chance with the love of his life.

If he fell on his face after this, then at least he would no longer have to live with regrets.

As he parked at the airport, his cell phone rang. Jenna's number came up on the caller ID. He considered waiting to call her back until he landed in Detroit, but he was dying to hear her voice.

He flipped open the phone. "Jenna?"

"Hi, Dylan," she said.

He swallowed. Should he tell her he was coming or just wait and surprise her after he landed?

"Are you already home?" he asked casually. He tried to come up with an apology for not calling before.

"As a matter of act, I'm not."

"Was your flight delayed?" The thought of that

made him frown. If hers was delayed because of weather, then his flight might be, as well, and he would hate having to wait any longer so see her.

"Actually, right now I'm at the optometrist's office."

"What do you mean?" His eyebrows drew together in confusion. She wasn't making any sense.

"To be specific, I'm at *your* office."

"What…?" he began again, but that lilt in her voice, the one that appeared whenever she thought she'd done something clever, cut through his confusion. "You didn't fly back to Detroit? Why?"

"I had to talk to you, so I showed up as a new patient. And if what your mom told me about your being at the airport is correct, then I'm guessing you wanted to talk to me."

Dylan smiled into the receiver. "That was supposed to be a surprise."

"And it would have been if you'd landed in Detroit and I was here in Indiana."

His thoughts raced as fast as his pulse pounded. He needed to see her now, to hear what she had to say and tell her what was in his heart, but fifty miles was too far and an hour was too long to wait. Suddenly an idea popped into his mind.

"Do you know the southbound rest stop on I-65? You know, the one about halfway between here and Markston?"

"Sure…I guess."

"Can you meet me there in half an hour?"

"I'll be there," she promised.

"And, Jenna." He paused until he was sure she would hear him. "I can't wait to see you."

Chapter Eighteen

When Jenna pulled into a spot near the rest stop's main entrance, Dylan's car was already there. Her heart was beating out a percussion solo, but she didn't want to waste time catching her breath. Since she was in a new rental car he might not recognize, she climbed out and hurried toward his SUV.

Before she reached it, his door flew open and he hopped down. He reached her in five long strides. Dylan closed his arms around her, parka and all, crushing her to his chest. She didn't even care if the hug was too tight to be comfortable. Then he pulled her hood back, and his mouth found hers in a kiss filled with adrenaline and joy.

"I can't believe you're here," she said when he pressed her to his shoulder again. Her arms clung tightly to his waist in an embrace she hoped would go on until they froze in front of the all tourists and truckers.

He did pull back far enough to look down at her face, but he didn't release her completely. "I can't believe I almost flew to Detroit."

"I can't believe we almost missed each other."

"So what's this about an optometry appointment?"

"It was kind of a grand gesture, but it was foiled. I wanted to be your patient because you helped me to see." She glanced at the snow-covered asphalt beneath her feet and then back up at him. "I guess it was kind of corny."

"Corny's good." He withdrew his preprinted boarding pass from the front pocket of his coat. "One grand gesture deserves another. Kind of a 'Gift of the Magi' thing."

"It was almost a Gift of the Mixups, but our moms saved us from that. I called my mom when you weren't at the office, and she called your mom and here we are."

"Meddling moms are a blessing," he agreed.

Jenna glanced around. They were still standing in the parking lot in each other's arms, and though they'd shared a kiss, neither had said anything that would change the situation they'd faced on New Year's Eve. She pointed to the opposite side of the lot. "I saw a nature trail over that way for walking dogs. Would you like to walk with me?"

Immediately, Dylan took her gloved hand and laced their fingers as he had the other night. That was a message in itself, but Jenna needed to say more and hoped to hear more, as well.

"I love you, Dylan," she said in a quiet voice as they walked along the path, the snow crunching beneath their feet.

He stopped walking, his breath appearing to hitch, and suddenly he was crushing her to his chest, holding her so tightly that she felt out of breath. He must have recognized her distress because he loosened his arms and took a small step back so he could look down at her. His eyes were suspiciously shiny.

"Do you know how long I've waited to hear that? I hoped for it and prayed for it, but I didn't really believe—" He stopped himself and grinned. "I really should have said it first, you know. I've had more years to feel it."

She couldn't help smiling at that, her heart already filling. "Oh. Okay. You go first."

Instead of speaking as they walked, he stopped and turned to face her. "Jenna, I love you. I can't remember a time when I didn't. I'm still afraid sometimes that I might lose you, but I can't allow that fear to keep us from having the future God has planned for us."

She stared into his eyes. "I love you, Dylan. You are my everything. You always were, even before I realized it. You never have to worry with me. My heart is yours…for keeps."

He pressed his lips to hers again in a warm, unhurried kiss. When he finally stepped back, Jenna didn't really need her parka anymore. He started chuckling, and when her eyes fluttered open, Jenna caught a few different dog walkers watching them curiously.

"There's a picnic area over here." He took her hand again and led her to a grouping of wooden picnic tables. He picked one and used his other gloved hand to wipe the snow off the top. Like a footman, he helped her up to sit on the table with her feet resting on the picnic bench.

When she was seated, he sank onto one knee in the snow. "Jenna Claire Scott, may I ask you a question?"

Was he really going to do what she thought he was

going to do? Her pulse pounding her ears, she couldn't speak, so she simply nodded.

"Would you like to go out to dinner and to a movie with me the next time you come to Markston?"

Instead of answering, she laughed out loud and shoved her hand through her hair. "Oh, dear," she said when the ripples of laughter finally calmed. "I thought you were going to propose to me before we even had our first date."

"So, what do you say?" He met her gaze. "To my question."

"Yes, Dylan, I would love to go on a date with you the next time I'm in town."

"Thank you." He popped up to kiss her lips once before he knelt again. "You know the knee of my pants is getting pretty wet here."

"Well, get up, then," she said, pulling up on his hand.

"Wait. I have some other questions for you."

"So ask." She was still giggling when she noticed that his expression had become serious.

"Jenna, you're my best friend. Will you also be my wife?"

Jenna coughed into her hand, her thoughts racing faster than the cars on the Indianapolis 500. "Are you sure there aren't other questions you want to ask me before that? Did I mention that we haven't been on a single date yet?"

"I could, but every other question I have is dependent on your answer to that question."

She thought about it for a second, and her pulse relaxed again. "I guess there probably isn't anything I could learn about you while bowling or eating pizza or playing miniature golf that I don't already know."

"So?" He quirked an eyebrow. "What do you say?" He glanced at the ground. "The knee's starting to go numb."

"Yes. Absolutely. I'll marry you. I never knew a real home until I found it in your arms."

Immediately he was up from the ground and kissing her as if he hadn't seen her in months. His kiss spoke of permanence and hope and the kind of friendship that is transformed by years into the love of a lifetime. When his mouth left hers, he kissed her forehead, nose and cheeks, all of which were starting to feel wind-burned.

When he stopped he climbed up and sat next to her on the tabletop. He put his arm around her, and she snuggled against his shoulder.

"Now what other questions did you have for me?"

"Will you live with me, be the mother of my children and grow old with me?"

"Yes times three. You were right. All of your other questions were dependent on the first one." She chuckled again. "Any more questions?"

"Will you fly in next weekend to go out with me?"

"Yes." She nodded for emphasis. "Anything else."

"Will you come the next weekend? And the next weekend? And the next? And the next?"

They were both laughing until he stopped and stared into her eyes. With a gentle touch, he lifted her chin and touched his lips to hers once more.

"My Jenna," he breathed, his words sounding like a prayer of thanksgiving.

"We'll have to do the distance thing for a while,

until I can get a transfer to Indianapolis International," she said, her mind suddenly in planning mode. "And then we'll have to plan the wedding."

Making affirmative sounds, Dylan kissed her between each comment.

"I'd like a simple one."

"Uh-huh."

"Just family and friends."

Dylan stopped and looked her in the eye. "Didn't you mention before that we haven't even gone on our first date?" He waited for her nod before he continued, "Then there's no rush. We'll do it in our time. So shh." He held his fingers to her lips. "Just kiss the guy, why don't you?"

She was happy to oblige there in the unromantic rest stop that had just become the most romantic place in the world. Her kiss offered him the promise of a future. A future with his best friend—and true love.

* * * * *

Dear Reader,

It's the Christmas season again, the time of year when I remind myself to focus on the serenity of the Christmas story without letting myself get lost in the frenzy of the season. And at some point during December, I usually forget that plan and enter the Christmas zone.

While in the zone, I shop and wrap like a madwoman, decorate as if my life depends on it and bake more cookies than my family could—or should—eat by New Year's Day. In the WEDDING BELL BLESSINGS miniseries, I based some of Amy Warren's over-the-top holiday celebrations on my own tendency to overdo.

I'm sure I'm not alone. Sometimes we as mothers feel obliged to put on a Christmas holiday that amazes our families, and in the process we lose out on the joy of Christmas. I wish for a different Christmas for all of us this year, one of quiet reflection. Instead of feeling overwhelmed, we can find hope and peace during this holy season.

I love hearing from readers and may be contacted through my Web site at www.danacorbit.com or through regular mail at P.O. Box 2251, Farmington Hills, MI 48333-2251.

Dana Corbit

QUESTIONS FOR DISCUSSION

1. Why does Dylan Warren immediately think he can relate to twins Connor and Ryan Denton? Did you ever experience a loss in your childhood? How did it affect you?

2. Why is Amy Warren so attached to her huge list of Christmas activities? How do her three sons feel about all those activities?

3. What was the final straw for Dylan that made him decide to end his friendship with Jenna? Do you believe it's better for two people to be friends first before beginning a love relationship?

4. Besides restoring her friendship with Dylan, what does Jenna want most? Does she find it?

5. How is Dylan different from the person Jenna used to know?

6. The Warrens and the Scotts decide to have a Christmas gift exchange even during their charity project, but the gifts must be homemade. What are some of the gifts they make for each other? Has your family ever had a gift exchange of home-made gifts and, if so, what did you make?

7. Reverend Boggs selects an unusual character from the cast of the nativity, Joseph, for his sermon

and then discusses how God spoke to biblical characters. Does God still speak to Christians today? In what ways?

8. What type of person was Jenna when she was younger? How did that affect the type of friendship she had with Dylan?

9. Even though Jenna is a new Christian, she is a work in progress, and she must learn to control some of the negative parts of her personality. What part does she find most difficult to control as she's trying to rebuild her relationship with Dylan?

10. What are the Christmas gifts that Amy Warren gives, or at least agrees to give, the Denton family from her own home? Have you ever given away something valuable to you to help someone else? Explain.

11. Why did Jenna not allow herself to acknowledge that Dylan had feelings for her when they were younger? What did she stand to lose?

12. What do the Scotts and the Warrens learn about the true meaning of Christmas through their efforts in adopting the Denton family over the holidays?

13. Why does Dylan believe that the Dentons still have what is most important even after they lose their possessions in the fire? How does that relate to what Jenna's family had, even through all of their moves?

14. Why do matchmakers Amy Warren and Trina Scott decide to set up Dylan with Caroline instead of Jenna?

15. What surprising lesson does Jenna teach Dylan about his faith?

Here is an exciting sneak preview of
TWIN TARGETS by Marta Perry,
the first book in the new 6-book
Love Inspired Suspense series
PROTECTING THE WITNESSES
available beginning January 2010.

Deputy U.S. Marshal Micah McGraw forced down the sick feeling in his gut. A law enforcement professional couldn't get emotional about crime victims. He could imagine his police chief father saying the words. Or his FBI agent big brother. They wouldn't let emotion interfere with doing the job.

"Pity." The local police chief grunted.

Natural enough. The chief hadn't known Ruby Maxwell, aka Ruby Summers. He hadn't been the agent charged with relocating her to this supposedly safe environment in a small village in Montana. He didn't have to feel responsible for her death.

"This looks like a professional hit," Chief Burrows said.

"Yeah."

He knew only too well what was in the man's mind. What would a professional hit man be doing in the remote reaches of western Montana? Why would anyone want to kill this seemingly inoffensive waitress?

And most of all, what did the U.S. Marshals Service have to do with it?

All good questions. Unfortunately he couldn't answer any of them. Secrecy was the crucial element that made the Federal Witness Protection Service so successful. Breach that, and everything that had been gained in the battle against organized crime would be lost.

His cell buzzed and he turned away to answer it. "McGraw."

"You wanted the address for the woman's next of kin?" asked one of his investigators.

"Right." Ruby had a twin sister, he knew. She'd have to be notified. Since she lived back east, at least he wouldn't be the one to do that.

"Jade Summers. Librarian. Current address is 45 Rock Lane, White Rock, Montana."

For an instant Micah froze. "Are you sure of that?"

"'Course I'm sure."

After he hung up, Micah turned to stare once more at the empty shell that had been Ruby Summers. She'd made mistakes in her life, plenty of them, but she'd done the right thing in the end when she'd testified against the mob. She hadn't deserved to end up lifeless on a cold concrete floor.

As for her sister…

What exactly was an easterner like Jade Summers doing in a small town in Montana? If there was an innocent reason, he couldn't think of it.

Ruby must have tipped her off to her location. That was the only explanation, and the deed violated one of the major principles of witness protection.

Ruby had known the rules. Immediate family could be relocated with her. If they chose not to, no contact was permitted—ever.

Ruby's twin had moved to Montana. White Rock was probably forty miles or so east of Billings. Not exactly around the corner from her sister.

But the fact that she was in Montana had to mean that they'd been in contact. And that contact just might have led to Ruby's death.

He glanced at his watch. Once his team arrived, he'd get back on the road toward Billings and beyond, to White Rock. To find Jade Summers and get some answers.

* * * * *

Will Micah get to Jade in time to save her from a similar fate?
Find out in TWIN TARGETS,
available January 2010
from Love Inspired Suspense.

Cheyenne Rhodes has come to Redemption, Oklahoma, to start anew, not to make new friends. But single dad Trace Bowman isn't about to let her hide her heart away. He just needs to convince Cheyenne that Redemption is more than a place to hide—it's also a way to be found....

Look for

Finding Her Way Home

by

Linda Goodnight

Available January wherever books are sold.

www.SteepleHill.com

Steeple Hill®

LI87571

LARGER-PRINT BOOKS!

GET 2 FREE LARGER-PRINT NOVELS PLUS 2 FREE MYSTERY GIFTS

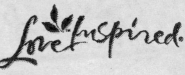

Larger-print novels are now available...

YES! Please send me 2 FREE LARGER-PRINT Love Inspired® novels and my 2 FREE mystery gifts (gifts are worth about $10). After receiving them, if I don't wish to receive any more books, I can return the shipping statement marked "cancel". If I don't cancel, I will receive 4 brand-new novels every month and be billed just $4.49 per book in the U.S. or $4.99 per book in Canada. That's a savings of over 30% off the cover price. It's quite a bargain! Shipping and handling is just 50¢ per book.* I understand that accepting the 2 free books and gifts places me under no obligation to buy anything. I can always return a shipment and cancel at any time. Even if I never buy another book, the two free books and gifts are mine to keep forever.

121 IDN EYLZ 321 IDN EYMF

Name	(PLEASE PRINT)	
Address		Apt. #
City	State/Prov.	Zip/Postal Code

Signature (if under 18, a parent or guardian must sign)

Mail to Steeple Hill Reader Service:

IN U.S.A.: P.O. Box 1867, Buffalo, NY 14240-1867
IN CANADA: P.O. Box 609, Fort Erie, Ontario L2A 5X3

**Are you a current subscriber of Love Inspired books
and want to receive the larger-print edition?
Call 1-800-873-8635 or visit www.morefreebooks.com.**

* Terms and prices subject to change without notice. Prices do not include applicable taxes. Sales tax applicable in N.Y. Canadian residents will be charged applicable provincial taxes and GST. Offer not valid in Quebec. This offer is limited to one order per household. All orders subject to approval. Credit or debit balances in a customer's account(s) may be offset by any other outstanding balance owed by or to the customer. Please allow 4 to 6 weeks for delivery. Offer available while quantities last.

Your Privacy: Steeple Hill Books is committed to protecting your privacy. Our Privacy Policy is available online at www.SteepleHill.com or upon request from the Reader Service. From time to time we make our lists of customers available to reputable third parties who may have a product or service of interest to you. If you would prefer we not share your name and address, please check here. ☐

LILP09

TITLES AVAILABLE NEXT MONTH

Available December 29, 2009

FINDING HER WAY HOME by Linda Goodnight
Redemption River

She came to Oklahoma to escape her past, but single dad
Trace Bowman isn't about to let Cheyenne Rhodes hide her
heart away. But will he stand by her when he learns the secret
she's running from?

THE DOCTOR'S PERFECT MATCH by Irene Hannon
Lighthouse Lane

Dr. Christopher Morgan is *not* looking for love. Especially with
Marci Clay. The physician and the waitress come from two very
different worlds. Worlds that are about to collide in faith and love.

HER FOREVER COWBOY by Debra Clopton
Men of Mule Hollow

Mule Hollow, Texas, is chock-full of handsome cowboys. Veterinarian
Susan Worth moves in, dreaming of meeting Mr. Right, who most
certainly is *not* the gorgeous rescue worker blazing through town...or
is he?

THE FAMILY NEXT DOOR by Barbara McMahon

Widower Joe Kincaid doesn't want his daughter liking their pretty
new neighbor. His little girl's lost too much already. And he doesn't
think the city girl will last a month in their small Maine town. But
Gillian Parker isn't what he expected.

A SOLDIER'S DEVOTION by Cheryl Wyatt
Wings of Refuge

Pararescue jumper Vince Reardon doesn't want to accept
Valentina Russo's heartfelt apologies for wrecking his motorcycle....
Until she shows this soldier what true devotion is really about.

MENDING FENCES by Jenna Mindel

Called home to care for her ailing mother, Laura Toivo finds herself in
uncertain territory. With the help of neighbor Jack Stahl, she'll learn
that life is all about connections, and that love is the greatest gift.

LICNMBPA1209